Dancing in the Darkness

Dancing in the Darkness

The Alpha God: Book 1

by
Lexa Luthor

Luthor Publishing
2023

This is a work of fiction. Names, characters, places, and incidents are the product of the author's imagination or are used fictitiously. Any resemblance to actual persons, living or dead, business establishments, events, or locales is entirely coincidental.

Dancing in the Darkness

Luthor Publishing
www.LexaLuthor.com

Editors:
RJ Creamer
Lila LaBine of LaBine Editorial

Cover Artist:
May Dawney of May Dawney Designs
www.maydawneydesigns.com

ISBN-13 (paperback):
978-1-7321153-8-5

ISBN-13 (ebook):
978-1-7321153-4-7

ISBN-13 (hardback):
978-1-952993-18-3

Second Edition – June 2023 – 01

Contents

Prologue

Charlie wiped the sweat from her brow after a long morning in the field. She had helped till the ground so that her adoptive parents could sew seeds. On the other side of the field, Laura and Zachary were close to finishing their end. Earlier the three of them had gone into the house to share lunch that their mother, Noelle, made them.

Adoptive mother, Charlie reminded herself.

About three years ago Charlie and her people had landed on Kander after their long journey from Earth. Charlie liked the planet, which was beautiful and reminded her of Earth, if not more on the colder side. The planet had longer, deeper winters than Earth. It was peculiar to Charlie, considering the planet circled two suns. The short summer season made it imperative that she and her adoptive family push to farm sooner in the springtime. Looking upward, Charlie confirmed the suns' location in the sky. They had passed their zenith and were headed south. The days were becoming longer as the tilted planet traveled around the suns.

"*Charlie, are you done?*" Zachary hollered in English across the field.

"*Yeah!*" Charlie turned to the two *pooren* next to her. They were large, wide mammals that reminded her of a cow that bred with a lion. They had horns, light-colored fur, and paws rather than hoofs. Both were females, which tended to be more docile compared to their male counterparts. She left their side and went to the two plows tied to the *pooren*. Charlie raised the moldboards so they wouldn't dig into the ground anymore.

She returned to the *pooren's* side, took their rein, and guided them both through the field. Her adoptive father, John, had traded for the *pooren* over the winter. Somehow John managed to arrange a deal with one of the local natives of the planet. Kander was populated by a humanoid race called the Kalmar. They hadn't taken it well when Earthlings arrived on their planet. Upon their arrival, fighting broke out, and death was a common occurrence even years later. At times, scrimmages happened between her people and the Kalmar. Peace was a fantasy.

Charlie met her adoptive siblings at the stable. Together, they unhooked their *pooren* and put them in their stalls for the day. Laura offered to feed and water them. Zachary thanked his sister, while Charlie was relieved to have a free afternoon. Tomorrow it would be her turn to muck the stalls.

Zachary followed Charlie to the house, which was closer to a wood cabin than a farmhouse. They traded banter about who tilled more farmland today. When they entered the house, Noelle greeted them as she continued her canning marathon.

"*What are you two up to?*" Noelle asked in English.

"*I'm going to watch movies,*" Zachary declared.

"*No!*" Noelle looked over her shoulder and pinned Zachary with a hard stare. "*You're going to read one of your summer books.*"

Charlie listened to their usual argument and tried not to snicker at the pitiful pout Zachary gave his mother. Thankfully she had already completed one of her two books for the summer reading requirement. Laura was almost done with her first one. But Zachary hadn't started his. Their teacher had warned them that their papers would be due on the first day of school.

"*Are you going to see Raine?*" Noelle asked when Charlie placed the dirty cup in the container.

"*Yes.*" Charlie shifted on her holey sock–covered feet. Her muddy boots were left at the door with everyone else's. "*We're meeting up in New Earth.*" She did her best to hold her adoptive mother's gaze. Noelle seemed to have a super power when it came to catching lies.

Noelle pulled out a fresh batch of jars from the pot of hot water. She set them aside and nodded. "*I expect you home by dark.*"

"*I will.*" Charlie looked over at Zachary, who was stuffing his face with a sandwich. In one year, he had grown quite a lot, and his appetite seemed never-ending. She looked back to Noelle, who gave her approval and handed her the wooden pass. Charlie didn't wait and ran to her room that she shared with Laura. She changed in record time and stuffed a few items into her leather knapsack. After slinging it on, she snatched her sheathed bowie knife and rushed out of the house while saying goodbye.

The walk to New Earth was about ten minutes. The road was a little muddy due to recent rain and snow melting from over the winter. She paused and hooked her bowie knife to the back of her faded jeans. The bowie knife was special to her, and she always carried it after her best friend gave it to her. From her oversized leather jacket, she fished out her dead mother's iPhone and earbuds. She popped in the earbuds and thumbed through the playlists that her mother had put together. Charlie didn't have the heart to delete them much less lose the bittersweet memories associated with the music.

From the Oldies playlist, she selected "Sweet Caroline," then nudged up the volume. She peered over her shoulder toward the Marshalls' farm and confirmed that no one was following her. Sometimes Laura or Zachary would chase after her and go to New Earth. But today she seemed to be on her own.

Charlie sang alongside Neil Diamond and skipped down the road. She was excited to spend the afternoon with her best friend, who would be waiting for her by the river. One year ago today they had met, and Charlie wanted to celebrate their friendship. As she came around a bend, she skidded to a walk and tightened her grip on her sack.

Two Earthlings were headed in Charlie's direction. They were dressed in military uniform and carried laser rifles on their backs. One of them pointed at Charlie, who relaxed once she recognized her. The Earthling settlement had a military division named the Liberator Force, which was spawned from the United States Air Force and the ship, the *Liberator*, that brought them here. Soldiers were called Liberatines, but everyone shortened it to Libs.

"*Hey, Charlie,*" Melissa Hoyt greeted in English.

The other Lib was a man who was younger than Melissa. He had a familiar face, but Charlie didn't know his name, nor did she care. With a critical eye, he studied Charlie from head to toe. "*Where are you headed to, kid?*"

"*It's the one road between the farms and the village. Where do you think, Cadet?*" Melissa shook her head at his terse attitude. "*How are you, Charlie?*" She ignored the other Lib's soft huff.

"*I'm good.*" Charlie reached into her pocket and produced the wooden pass that Noelle gave her. She held it toward Melissa, but the cadet snatched it from her. "*I'm headed to New Earth to see Raine.*"

Melissa nodded and glanced at the cadet. He had produced a tablet and scanned a tiny chip hidden inside the wooden pass. "*How is Raine? I haven't seen her lately.*"

"*She's been busy.*" Charlie didn't offer much else because her friendship with Raine had cracked a little. The idea that she might lose the friendship left a dull ache in her heart.

"*Hmmm.*" Melissa yanked the pass from the cadet and returned it to Charlie. "*I heard she went with a crew into Gaular for supplies. But they should be back by now.*" She studied Charlie for a long moment. The town of Gaular was an hour's hike from New Earth and had plenty of supplies compared to the smaller villages around them. The problem was that Gaular was a Kalmar town. In the early days, battles and fights took place there. The Earthlings continued to go out of necessity, and a thin line of tolerance had developed from the local Kalmar. But there was never a guarantee that fighting wouldn't happen again for the smallest of reasons.

"*If she isn't, I'll wait for her.*" Charlie had no plans to see Raine. Her stomach twisted after lying yet again, but she had to.

"*Be careful.*" Melissa patted Charlie on the shoulder, then she and the cadet continued their patrol.

Charlie looked over her shoulder and watched the Libs. She had always liked Melissa, who had kept an eye on her ever since Earth's destruction. Melissa had been an airman in the Air Force and later converted to a Liberatine, always devoted to duty.

The rest of the walk to New Earth was uneventful. Charlie made it to the market before it closed for the day. She visited one of the food vendors and was lucky enough to score a chocolate bread loaf. For the past year, New Earth had started receiving goods from off-world alien traders, who were willing to land by the settlement and exchange goods. Due to the new relations, a few hard-to-find items were brought back to their Earthling culture, such as technology, specific foods, plant seeds, and medical supplies. Among those goods was chocolate.

After Charlie traded with the merchant, she wrapped the small loaf in a piece of cloth and tied it. She tucked it into her bag and hurried through New Earth, heading out of town but on a different road. She wouldn't have to travel far before she could duck off the road and make her way to the river. Much to her chagrin, a group was headed toward her and had spotted her. She should have traveled through the woods, but it was faster to use the road for a while first before going into the woods.

Slowing her pace, Charlie hastened to devise an excuse for why she was on the road. They may not say anything to her, or they might stop her. Being a kid often lent to a lot of questions and concerns. The adults in their settlement seemed to forget that most kids survived outer space and had grown up a long time ago.

"*Hey, Charlie!*"

Cringing, Charlie cursed at her bad luck and forced a smile. "*Hey, Raine.*" She stepped aside when the returning crew from Gaular trekked by. They pulled loaded carts of supplies. "*How'd it go in Gaular?*"

"*Better than last time.*" Raine hooked a hand across the strap of her laser rifle. She was over three years older than Charlie, at least in Earth years. Similar to Charlie, she was a kid, yet she carried a gun. Once a person reached fourteen, they were allowed to train and carry a laser weapon. On her fourteenth birthday, Raine had entered the training program, passed it, and joined the crew missions to go to Gaular. Raine might join the Libs on her eighteenth birthday.

But Charlie stayed clear of the Liberatines, the fighting, and the politics.

"*That's good,*" Charlie said and tried to act normal. "*What are you doing when you get back to New Earth?*"

"*Early dinner, then I might go see what Silva is doing.*" Raine moved to the side while the rest of the crew continued their walk to New Earth. She canted her head and asked, "*Where are you headed?*"

Charlie shrugged and replied, "*I was going for a walk. I wanted to see if the river has defrosted enough for fishing.*"

Raine snorted and shook her head. "*You and fishing.*" She had heard several of Charlie's fishing stories from when Charlie went with her dad. There were even a few videos on Charlie's iPhone thanks to her mother capturing those moments. "*Be careful out there.*" She took a step away and said, "*Come have dinner with me when you're done.*" The invite was sweet and tugged at Charlie's heart.

Swallowing hard, Charlie walked backward and said, "*See you, Rae Rae.*" She turned and heard Raine's farewell. Charlie picked up the pace, then darted into the woods once she ensured that no one was around her. Raine was aware of Charlie's fishing hole, but she didn't know where on the river Charlie fished. And for good reason.

Charlie traveled through the woods, trying to fight the urge to run. Her friend would wait for her even if she was late. She came upon the river and turned to her right, following the river farther downstream. After another five minutes of walking through brush and hopping over fallen branches, she approached the meeting spot. Long ago a huge tree had fallen across the river, creating a natural bridge between two worlds. Seated on the fallen tree was a female who was a little older than Charlie. She smiled when Charlie came into view.

"*Turen, Dorlon!*" Charlie greeted and waved a hand. Her mind switched from English to the native tongue of the Kalmar. Her people had dubbed the language as Kalmarese while the Kalmar called English Earthlang.

"*Turen!*" Dorlon launched off the tree, lifted her dress above her ankles, and ran toward Charlie. At the last second, she let go of her dress and launched herself into Charlie's waiting arms. "It's so good to see you."

Charlie squeezed her best friend and hefted her off the ground, earning a delighted squeal. "I missed you too." A year ago, she and Dorlon couldn't speak beyond saying hello, yes, and no. But they taught each other their own language. Charlie hadn't mastered Kalmarese, but she was apt at it more than Dorlon was at English.

Once Dorlon was on her feet again, she switched to English and said, "*Happy friendiversary!*"

Charlie smiled and threw her arms in the air. "*Happy friendiversary!*" She and Dorlon hugged again, then they went about making a campfire to keep warm on a cool spring day. Dorlon had taught Charlie how to build and start fires with the natural resources around them. Charlie had once been spoiled by her father and his matches.

"How was plowing?" Dorlon asked and took a seat beside Charlie in front of the fire. They each used a foldable stool that Charlie had snuck out here one day. When they were done visiting, they hid them up in a tree, using vines.

"It was tiring." Charlie was in fact sore, having to manipulate the plows or move large rocks out of the way. "My stepfather said we tomorrow off before we put in seeds." She grumbled at her messy Kalmarese, but Dorlon often understood her.

Dorlon nodded and tucked her hands between her knees. She wore a jacket that went past her waist for extra warmth. "The ice and snow are gone. It's a good time to plow." When Charlie offered her a container of water, she drank from it.

"How your day?" Charlie asked and received the metal bottle back. She took a large gulp from it.

"Good. Alsace helped me rebuild the garden beds." Dorlon studied her hands in her lap. She was a few years younger than her brother, Alsace. Their household consisted of her, Alsace, and their father. "I promised my sire that I would grow more for him to sell at the market."

To sell, then drink away the profits, Charlie silently concluded after what Dorlon had told her in the past. She placed a hand on Dorlon's knee. "You are good growing vegetables and herbs. I sure you can."

Dorlon nodded and sat quiet for a moment. She and her brother worked hard to keep their heads above poverty. Their father was little to no help. "I know." She closed her open hands and looked at Charlie. "We'll be able to fish soon." Her smile reappeared.

"I can't wait!" Charlie looked forward to them sitting on the tree bridge and casting their lines. The white fish were between twelve to sixteen inches long. Sometimes they would cook one that day, and other times they took them home. The fish's flavor reminded Charlie of the trout she caught with her father.

"You said we're going to celebrate our *friendiversary*?" Dorlon had a hopeful gaze and waited for what Charlie had in mind.

"*Ja!*" Charlie agreed and grabbed her sack. She dug around until she found the special treat. "You remember I said *chocolate*?" Pulling out her prize, she held out the wrapped bread and started to undo the tie.

"Oh." Dorlon gushed when Charlie presented the uncovered bread. "It is so dark like *tunjer* bread."

"Smell it." Charlie held it closer to Dorlon's face.

Dorlon pressed her hands against Charlie's and guided it closer to her nose. She had a stronger sense of smell than humans did. After one inhale, she turned her big eyes onto Charlie. "Wow! I want to try it."

Grinning, Charlie placed the bread in her lap, with the cloth spread out under it. She retrieved her bowie knife and ensured it was clean enough.

"Do you always carry it?" Dorlon asked and watched Charlie cut several slices from the loaf.

"*Ja*," Charlie replied and set the dirty blade on the sheath in case Dorlon wanted more bread later. Dorlon had gifted her the knife over the winter, then shown Charlie how to clean and sharpen it. "Here." She handed a piece of bread to her friend. "You try first."

Dorlon took a bite and chewed once before she went still. She covered her mouth with a hand, but the brightness of her eyes gave away her awe. "*Chocolate?*"

After a soft snort, Charlie nodded and asked, "What think?" She ate a small morsel, testing its flavor. The chocolate was distinct but not overpowering, especially in a bread. But it was new to Dorlon.

"I like it." Dorlon bit off a larger chunk and hummed while she ate it. By her third mouthful, she wiggled back and forth on the stool. "I think I love it."

Charlie laughed and popped the last piece of her slice into her mouth. "I knew you would." Trading her month's allowance for the bread was worth it. "It hard to get *chocolate*."

"How did you get it?"

After a shrug, Charlie replied, "I traded for it."

"You're lucky alien traders come to New Earth." Dorlon grabbed another slice, cramming it into her mouth. Alien traders went to large towns and cities throughout Kander, but not villages like Dorlon's.

Charlie giggled and adored her friend's new love for chocolate. She should have traded for it sooner, but saving it for the anniversary of their friendship was a great way to celebrate it. Her friendship with Raine had fractured, but Charlie was grateful to have forged a friendship with Dorlon. They may be Kalmar and Earthling, but they were family to each other.

Dorlon was stuffed after eating a third slice. She reached over for Charlie's water bottle, causing her jacket's sleeve to shimmy up her forearm. A dark welt revealed itself and caught Charlie's attention.

Charlie snared her friend's hand and gently tugged the jacket higher. The welt mark was one of three others that went the length of Dorlon's forearm. A strong sting started behind her eyes, but she blinked it away. "Dor, what happened?" Without asking, she knew who had hurt her friend.

Dorlon pulled her hand free and pushed the jacket's sleeve back down. "Later," she whispered and picked up the bottle. "I don't want to spoil our special day." After a long drink, she handed the bottle to Charlie, who took a swallow next.

"*Perka gi,*" Charlie apologized and set the water bottle aside. She rewrapped the bread, which gave her a moment to compose herself. It wasn't the first time Charlie had found bruising on her friend's body. She wasn't a violent person, but Charlie wanted to use her knife on Dorlon's sire. After a sigh, she looked at her friend and suggested, "Summer coming. We could go."

"*Joh,*" Dorlon denied. She folded her arms in her lap, cradling the injured one. "I can't leave Alsace with him."

Charlie wanted to argue that Alsace could handle himself. She also admired Dorlon's closeness to her brother, who attempted to protect her. But he couldn't always shield Dorlon. She grumbled and made a second attempt. "What about other family?"

Dorlon plucked at her light brown dress. "My aunt is the closest one." She looked to Charlie and explained, "She and her mate live on a farm. They have a son and twins."

"Twins?" Charlie was intrigued by the new information about Dorlon's extended family.

"*Ja*, they're about five or maybe six now." Dorlon lost her tiny smile. "I haven't met them. I doubt I ever will." She leaned forward and stared at the fire. "I can't leave Alsace," she repeated and rubbed her hands together.

Charlie let it go rather than push her friend. Some time later, she would try again until she could convince Dorlon that it was safer to leave home than stay. Maybe they could figure out how to make a safe life together. Charlie's human scent would give her away to any Kalmar, but there might be a way to pass as a Kalmar by masking her scent.

"I'm fine." Dorlon offered a smile, as if reading Charlie's thoughts. But the dimness in her eyes left a knot in Charlie's stomach. Dorlon picked up on it with her keen senses and said, "Come here." She chuckled when Charlie scrambled over. Without hesitation, Charlie plopped into her friend's lap, hooked an arm around her shoulders, and snuggled with Dorlon, who let out a contented rumble that calmed them both.

Charlie rested her head against Dorlon's shoulder and breathed in her distinct scent. She'd come to learn how the Kalmar used their scents and pheromones to broadcast different messages. Charlie might be human, but she responded to a Kalmar's scent all the same. "One day we move away from this."

"One day," Dorlon murmured and tightened her arms around Charlie. Her breaths were slow and deep, relaxing them both.

Charlie smiled and closed her eyes. When she first arrived on Kander, she was relieved to be free of the spaceship. But then the bloodshed started and put Charlie in a constant state of fear. Later on, she and Dorlon had crossed paths, giving Charlie a shred of hope and sanity. Their friendship was a secret and could cost one of them, or both, if their people found out.

"I love you, Dor," Charlie whispered in perfect Kalmarese. Their friendship might be seen as forbidden, but it meant change was possible. If they could build a relationship, then their races could find peace. She wanted to believe that their friendship might somehow change the future of their people.

After a warm purr, Dorlon nuzzled into Charlie's neck. In English, she responded, "*I love you too. Always.*"

Chapter 1

From the pilot's seat, Charlie continued singing one of her favorite songs and navigated the spaceship *Pacifica* closer to the broken moon Lerto. The rocky, split sphere orbited an uninhabitable gaseous planet in a quiet solar system near the center of the Milky Way galaxy. As the *Pacifica* slowed, the dark moon's artificial gravity hugged the ship's hull.

Behind the captain's chair, Charlie sensed one of her crewmembers standing over her shoulder, but nothing had to be said about their current location. After a minute, the ship's flight systems were set to standby now that they were settled into the moon's orbit for the next several hours.

In the copilot's seat, Raakor, the second crewmember, was busy tapping the flight control's touch panel a few times before he brushed a visible piece of bionic tech embedded in his neck. The tech in his purple skin flashed a soft red, indicating he was connected to the ship's system.

After a glance at the screen, Charlie confirmed the artificial handshake between Raakor and the ship before she shut down the flight and navigation modules. From behind the captain's chair, Starr folded her arms and spoke in an alien language called Jero. "*I hope we're going down for drinks.*"

Charlie smirked and lowered the music from the control panel, then spun the seat around to face Starr. "*Yes, considering tomorrow's meeting on Kander.*"

"*How far are we from Kander?*"

"*Almost three parse lumens from Kander. We hop over one solar system.*" Charlie studied Starr, who was keeping it together despite tomorrow's pending meeting. "*Thanks for doing this, Starr.*"

After a low grunt, Starr glared out the front window at the broken moon. "*Stills are stills. We need the money. Fates know the* Pacifica *could use an overhaul.*" Raakor's huff brought her attention to him.

Charlie scanned the interior of the ship and agreed that it needed maintenance now that wiring was exposed, paint was peeling, doors were squeaking, and touch panels were glitchy. And similar to Starr, she was struggling with returning to Kander after so long and tried to keep her emotions in check. If nothing else, a few good beers on Lerto would settle her nerves. "*Want to jettison in ten?*"

"*Sure.*" Starr canted her head and tapped Raakor's chair. "*You coming with us?*"

Raakor was silent and seemed to be considering his options.

Charlie knew he wasn't fond of drinking, but this time she wanted him to join them. "*We should talk more about this mission. And practice our Kalmarese more too.*" Earlier she had suggested they switch to speaking in Kalmarese so they were ready for the mission.

Raakor gave a soft sigh but nodded and stood up from the copilot seat. In Kalmarese, he said, "See you in ten." He slipped past Starr without another word and vanished deeper into the ship.

Starr folded her arms, revealing her thick biceps highlighted by her short-sleeved shirt. "Raakor already know about the Kalmar people." At least she took seriously Charlie's suggestion about practicing the Kalmar's native tongue. Unlike Charlie, her Kalmarese was rough, but Starr had learned the language during her childhood.

"Not enough," Charlie argued in Kalmarese. "I want to make sure he doesn't accidentally piss off an

Alpha, especially *the* Alpha." She believed in Raakor's ability to process many difficult situations, until it came to feelings. Logic rarely worked well against emotions, especially when it came to the Kalmar people—their possible new client.

Starr nodded before heading out of the cockpit.

Charlie followed her friend through the ship and entered the row of aft cabin doors. She, Raakor, and Starr had separate quarters, while the other two remained empty for the occasional guest.

Once in her quarters, Charlie changed out of her run-down canvas pants and black shirt. She put on a pair of tight, weathered jeans that had cost her more stills than she cared to tell anyone. Next was a deep-red shirt that hugged her curves, but her black leather jacket hid it all. After pocketing a lectra gun inside the jacket, she ducked into the head, which lit up and revealed the mirror over the sink.

From her reflection, Charlie decided time and space were indeed catching up to her now that she was around thirty-two in Earth years. Her wavy hair had once been golden like sunshine, but due to life in outer space, it was now an amber shade. Besides a few freckles over her smooth cheekbones, she had rather pale and square features. After pulling a brush through her tangled strands, Charlie applied a soft shade of red lip gloss, then hurried out of the cabin.

With a techbit in hand, Charlie checked her current balance of stills, and the low number made her grouse. It looked like her dinner would consist of liquids. Starr was right that they needed the stills from this upcoming job, or they would be hard-pressed to survive any further.

After a grumble or two, the techbit's screen shut off, and Charlie tucked it inside her leather jacket. She peered out the round window and studied the fractured moon, which was dark other than a patch lit up by the moon's residents. Her thoughts drifted, much like the ship, until heavy boot steps made her look at her crew.

"Ready?" Starr asked, continuing to use Kalmarese.

Charlie answered by approaching one of the two shuttles, which could seat four people each. They would take a shuttle to the moon's surface. They could land the *Pacifica* on Lerto, but they would incur a docking fee. Shuttles were much smaller and often weren't charged for landing at a docking location.

Starr grunted when Charlie picked a shuttle. There was a different air around her than usual. Under the bay's dim light, Starr's short dark hair had a silver hue, and her brown eyes were more blown than normal. Due to her biology, she was tall and had a bulky frame, which made it easy for her to act as Charlie's muscle. Unlike Charlie, she wore gray pants and a heavy dark shirt that hugged her muscular figure. A thick leather belt hung around her waist and held a lectra handgun.

"You look damn human," Starr remarked, then loaded into the vessel from the copilot's side.

Raakor ducked under the rear passenger door and sat in the bucket seat.

After getting into the pilot's spot, Charlie grinned and stated, "Because I am."

Starr rolled her eyes and buckled up as the shuttle came to life. "Does not mean you need be fucking obvious." Most times, her Kalmarese was decent, but at times she missed words. Charlie had spoken Kalmarese longer than Starr. Raakor had it the easiest since he could download the language, which Charlie had to scrounge up from a merchant.

Charlie glanced at Starr and noticed the soft shine in Starr's brown eyes. "It's Lerto, and they have no laws against humans." Hell. There were only two laws on Lerto—no murder and no rape.

"Not yet," Starr muttered.

The dashboard beeped, indicating it was safe to reverse the shuttle out of the bay of the *Pacifica.* Charlie steered the shuttle while she considered Starr's deteriorating mood, which could affect the meeting tomorrow. Maybe it was the pending meeting that was rattling Starr, but Charlie had a sixth sense about Starr's biology.

Once the shuttle was out of the bay, Charlie flicked several switches and started navigating toward the moon. "Don't tell me you're flaring, Starr." From the thick silence, she scowled at her and snapped, "This is really, I mean, *really* bad timing."

"It early for some reason," Starr argued and snarled.

With white knuckles, Charlie gripped the helm controls and said, "We are going to Kander tomorrow and if they—"

"I know!" Starr fumed and had fire in her eyes that silenced Charlie, for now.

Charlie held her tongue and tried focusing on the flight to Lerto, but she considered Starr's hybrid body due to her bi-species background. As half human and half Kalmar, Starr faced prejudice on their former home planet of Kander. There was less bigotry in outer space, except when the occasional cutthroat wanted to collect on an outdated bounty for Starr's hybrid nature. After a low huff, she spotted the landing pads at Lerto's ship port. She and Starr had gone to Lerto over forty times in their two years together.

But Raakor, who remained silent in the back, had been to the moon a handful of times. He preferred to keep to himself and worked on different projects or dedicated his time to ship maintenance. In the past year, he had become an essential asset to Charlie's team.

The flight to the landing port was easy, and Charlie lowered the shuttle with expert skill. She and the crew walked to the local watering hole in the city. The dirty streets were lit by torches, and every humanoid and not-so-humanoid species passed by them. Charlie received most of the starcs and heard the whispers behind her back, which was normal. Starr walked closer to her, a clear indication of her flare-up.

Charlie downed two shots at the bar, then ordered a beer when they sat down at a table. Starr gulped her first beer but sipped on the second one while Raakor nursed a Whirly ale, his one favorite from what Charlie could tell.

For a moment, Charlie stared at Raakor and thought about his time since joining her crew. Raakor was huge and had a rich purple hue to his skin, typical of his species. There wasn't a single hair on him, but tattoos decorated his body. He was always shirtless but kept his dark jacket zipped up, hiding many of his old scars. His gray pants had oily splotches, and his thick-heeled boots made him even taller. Raakor could fight when necessary, and Charlie had nicknamed him the Gentle Giant.

From their small corner, the three mercenaries enjoyed the view of the busy bar and hums of conversation in various languages. The most common language among the customers was Jero, a universal language from the oldest race in the galaxy, the Jerothian. There were at least eight different species between the tables and stools. Two bartenders, who were twin Rath species, worked the long bar while a dozen servers rushed around to bring drinks or food.

At times, the place could be dank due to it being built into a cliffside, but Charlie liked the natural gray stone walls all around them. Gazing up, she smiled at the shiny moonstones that peeked through the rock ceiling. The unusual stones were natural to the moon and acted as tiny mirrors, reflecting any light, such as the torches that lined the walls. In the center was a round fire pit that helped to heat and dry out things, on a good day.

As Charlie's crew enjoyed their drinks, different people approached them and solicited offers for the night. Charlie waited to see if Starr would accept any. Many species throughout the galaxy could often sense Starr's flare-ups, and it made her an easy target for prostitutes. They assumed her natural biological need to reproduce overcame her better senses when she was in a flare. One fair-haired, emerald-skinned beauty had caught Starr's attention, but the price had been too high. The next person was a furry creature from the Jerhath race that Charlie kept calling a bat.

Starr waited until the Jerhath was gone before she leaned over the table toward Charlie. "He smell like rotten eggs."

Charlie choked on her sweet alcohol and asked, "You were that close to him?" For once, speaking in another language afforded them a little privacy. Few in outer space spoke, much less knew of, Kalmarese.

Raakor shook his head and finished off the ale.

"He practically in my lap," Starr replied and huffed but looked to her boss. "What time the meeting again?"

Charlie shifted her mindset to business, wanting to ensure both her crewmen were prepared for tomorrow. She leaned against the table when Raakor answered the question. "Eleven hundred Kander time."

"Did you read through the history doc I put together?" Charlie asked him. She needed him to be somewhat familiar with the Kalmar species.

Raakor folded his arms and nodded. "Uploaded to my brain and processed." He was from the Hurr race, which were steeped in technology. Like other Hurr, he had a bionic chip attached to his brain, allowing data to be downloaded or uploaded rather than having to read or watch to learn.

Charlie was pleased with Raakor's preparedness. He did seem to have a strong grasp of their language. She shifted mental gears back to the main topic. "We need to go over the Kalmar and how they work."

"I understand the Kalmar," Raakor declared.

"Then I want to know what you know," Charlie said. "Because if any of us"—she cut her attention to Starr, then back to Raakor—"screw this up then we're fucked. But if we get this job, we could stand to make out really good."

"Really well," Starr corrected.

Charlie smacked Starr's forearm and looked at Raakor again. "No other mercs have been hired by Kalmar, *ever*."

"But they selected us," Raakor countered.

"Maybe find out why later." Starr shrugged.

Nodding, Charlie sat back in the chair and said, "Tell me what you know."

After an exasperated sigh, Raakor slouched against the chair and folded his arms, showing his rich violet skin that reflected the bar's low light. "Kander is a terrestrial planet that is eighty-seven point six percent land and the rest water. It's been inhabited since—"

"Wait," Charlie cut off and waved a hand. "I don't need the planet's dating profile. What do you know about the Kalmar themselves?"

Raakor finished off his drink, then set the empty mug to the sidc. "Thcy'rc a biped humanoid species who have a strong sense of smell, superior night vision, and they age slower than other humanoid species. They are divided into two types: one is Alpha and the other is Omega. The Alphas are generally larger and stronger and known for being aggressive, boorish, and volatile. The Omegas are considered more reasonable, submissive, and nurturing but can be protective. Physically they are smaller than the Alphas." He paused when Charlie nodded at him; he grumbled and continued relaying what he knew. "They typically mate for life after the Alpha ruts, knots, and impregnates an Omega who's in heat."

"Good," Charlie praised. "But don't let the whole Omega's submissive thing go to your head. They're actually feistier than what everyone thinks." She glanced over at Starr, who was drinking her beer. "What do you know about their government?" she asked him next.

"The planet is controlled by a single monarch called the High Commander."

"The Kalmar also call him Kal," Charlie said.

Raakor had a curious glow in his eyes and the tilt of his head prompted Charlie.

"Every High Commander is called Kal," Charlie revealed. "It's like every Roman Emperor being called Caesar after…" She faltered because she realized Raakor knew little about Earth's history. "Anyway, the Kal is always an Alpha, and they had a new Kal take power about…" She looked to Starr for help.

"About eight orbits ago," Starr supplied. "During the messy civil war."

Raakor hummed low and nodded once. "A war started by the Earthlings landing and settling on Kander."

"*Ja*," Charlie agreed. "It was a fucking mess." She frowned and muttered, "Probably still is." Most of her childhood memories from Kander were horrible, but she refocused on the conversation and said, "The Kal is also considered their god."

"Indirectly," Starr debated and took over the religious explanation of the planet. "Myth that their god, Kalatas, select an Alpha, come down, and merge with the Alpha so they can rule together. It stay inside the Alpha until death, then Kalatas choose another."

Raakor huffed low and looked between Starr and Charlie before asking, "Is it true?"

"It's probably bullshit," Charlie whispered, then took a last huge swallow of her drink, finishing it. "We should get back." She stood up when yet another curious individual neared their table, and she groaned at the damn species.

"*Humansss rarely come here,*" a Gyr said in Jero. "*What'sss left of them.*" The Gyr's scaly, iridescent skin reflected the bar's light, and it blinked with dual eye slits.

Charlie opened her mouth but was cut off by Starr's chair scraping against the stone floor. At her side, Starr rose about a foot higher than her. Charlie could handle any insults, slurs, or attacks about her dying kind, especially with her quick wit and trigger finger. But tonight, she allowed Starr to handle it, and amusement glowed in her blue eyes.

"*And there'll be less of you left if you bother us further.*" Starr commanded the Gyr's attention, along with the others in the bar. She was taller than most races in the galaxy, and her bulk intimidated many.

Raakor made his presence known next, standing almost as tall as Starr. He fisted his hands at his sides.

Charlie sighed at the Gyr's glare on Starr. A low hiss from the Gyr told her that it was assessing Starr in finer detail. As the heartbeats passed, the Gyr submitted to Starr's dominance, and it somewhat disappointed Charlie. Over the years, she had grown accustomed to Starr's aggressive personality and never yielded to it.

"*A Kalman,*" the Gyr said, in disdain.

Charlie flinched when the Gyr used the slur for Starr's mixed-species background. Not everyone was familiar with a Kalman, but being this close to Kander, it wasn't a surprise. She reached into her jacket for the handgun in case a brawl started between Starr and the Gyr. From a stolen glance, she caught a dangerous smile from Starr.

"*Call me that again, and I'll rip your tongue out.*" Starr raised her hands, ready to launch herself across the table.

The Gyr hissed again but took one step back and said, "*There's a bounty on you half-breeds.*"

Charlie rolled her eyes at the mention of the old bounty. She folded her arms with the black laser gun in front of her chest. "*And why do you think she's still alive?*" She smiled when the nervous Gyr looked at her again but with wide eyes. Many species didn't expect a human to have any skills with Jero. "*I'd back off.*" She tilted her head as the Gyr reversed farther, bumping into Raakor, then hurried off without another word.

Starr snorted low.

Charlie lowered her arms and touched Starr's stiff shoulder. "*We should go back to the shuttle.*" They left the bar after paying the tab, went to their shuttle, and loaded into it.

The ride back to the *Pacifica* was thick with tense air and Starr's heavy breaths. Charlie rubbed the space between her eyes and realized the next day was going to be hell. Of all the times for Starr to flare up, right now was the worst. The Celestial Fates were toying with them, and it was the best explanation for such horrible luck. Charlie considered asking Starr to stay behind on the ship tomorrow, but her imagination had already played out the fight.

Once back on the ship, Starr stumbled out of the confines of the shuttle with Raakor at her side. She clutched her lower belly but allowed Charlie to touch her forehead.

"You're burning up," Charlie whispered. "Help me get Starr to her quarters." Together, she and Raakor managed Starr's bulkier weight and headed to the cabins.

Once inside, Starr slid out of their arms and into the waiting bed.

"I'll take care of her," Charlie told Raakor, who slipped out of the cabin without a word. She then came to the bedside and offered, "I'll stay with you."

"*Joh.* I'll be fine after I take the meds." Starr stumbled when she stood, still clutching her stomach. The deep lines across her brow indicated her growing agony from the flare-up's arrival. The alcohol seemed to have done little to stall it.

"Just stay there."

For a tick, Starr's mouth hung open with a dying protest. She nodded and sunk into the bed. They both knew the reality of Starr's flare-up, thanks to her Kalmar father and a human mother. As a hybrid, she faced different inherited qualities from both of her parents and often disdained it. She escaped Kander as a kid and found direction after meeting Charlie and becoming a mercenary.

Long ago, Charlie had learned about Starr's flare-ups, which mimicked an Omega's heat but more subtle. Like an Omega's heat, the flare-up was both painful and taxing on Starr and left her in a sexual haze, always on alert for a potential mate. Unlike an Omega, Starr's flare-ups tended to follow a consistent schedule like a human female's menstruation cycle. Medication helped dull and make the flare-up bearable.

After shaking her head, Charlie rubbed her forehead and said, "This is bad timing, Starr." She debated whether to switch back to Jero for Starr's sake.

While on her back, Starr growled low and closed her eyes. "It be fine."

"Raakor and I can handle the meeting." Charlie tensed when Starr shot upright. Her friend's response wasn't unexpected, but Charlie was the captain and leader. She had the final decision.

"*Joh*," Starr argued, and her dark eyes drilled into Charlie. "If you think I let you go alone to a planet full of fuck Alphas, then you—"

"I'm not going alone." Charlie rushed into the bathroom, locating the medicine and filling a cup of water from the sink. "We can handle it." She handed over the items to Starr.

"Raakor is good with wrench, not gun." Starr then groused before popping the pills and washing them down with the water.

Charlie bit her tongue because it was true. She brought Starr into her crew because of her brawn and common sense. Raakor was indeed large and looked menacing, but he preferred to keep a low-profile during fights. He was an excellent mechanic, copilot, and backup.

After a sigh, Charlie tossed the cup into the sink with a dramatic force and started for the front door. "Don't fuck it up for us." She was pushing her luck by challenging Starr, who was slipping into days of sexual frustration and pain.

"Don't you fuck up," Starr countered.

Huffing low, Charlie nodded once and nudged the door open. "See you in a few." She went to her quarters and was happy to have the space from her now overbearing crewmember. The damn flare-ups were an inconvenience at times, but she accepted that part of Starr when she took her on. They both had important skills that they brought to the team, and Charlie damn well hoped that Starr could focus enough during this crucial mission. They stood to make a lot of stills and earn some fame at the end, if they succeeded.

Chapter 7

Together, Charlie and Raakor controlled the *Pacifica* from the cockpit and maneuvered the ship closer to the beautiful planet named Kander. The terrestrial sphere was one of the three other planets in the tiny solar system that had two stars. In the distance, a floating metal object reflected the solar light from the two suns, but Charlie did her best to ignore it. Once they had the ship floating near Kander's moon, they stared at the planet that awoke unspoken memories.

Kander was over ten percent larger than Earth, by Charlie's estimation, or at least what once was Earth. Kander also had more landmass, which made it a greener and browner planet than Earth with its former vast oceans. At either pole were soft white caps of water, locked as ice for millennia. But the most unusual feature about the solar system was the dual suns, where one sun acted as the primary and the second weaker one hovered near it.

"How long until meeting?" Starr asked in Kalmarese as she entered the cockpit.

Raakor was busy with the touch panel in the copilot's seat.

With a glance at Kander's local time on the control panel, Charlie replied, "In forty-five minutes local time." Starr's heavy sigh made Charlie reconsider whether Starr should join them on Kander. "Maybe you should—"

"*Joh.*"

The cockpit swelled with tension, and Charlie contained her eye roll. Forty-five minutes was enough time to get down to the ground, but none of them were rushing to the shuttle bay. She climbed to her feet and ordered, "Come on. We can't be late."

Starr led the way to the shuttle and sniffed when Charlie passed her. "You showered?"

Charlie knew it was rhetorical and replied, "I'm not taking any risks." The Kalmar could scent anything, from an alien to a bug. The last thing they needed was for the Kalmar to think that Charlie, Starr, or Raakor were lovers thanks to their close quarters. The tight confines of their ship forced much of their scents to commingle. Starr disliked that her hybrid scent was enough to stir trouble, but mixed scents with a hybrid could cause an argument.

They couldn't leave the possible job to chance, no matter how small.

Raakor pretended to sniff himself and lifted an eyebrow ridge at Starr.

"You smell like oil," Starr promised. She rolled her eyes when Raakor flashed a grin, then climbed into the vessel's open door and buckled up for the ride to the planet below.

Charlie patted the outdoor hull, which was looking a bit shabby. They needed those stills. But like the *Pacifica*, the shuttle was a sturdy piece of thick alloy, which had always protected them. Once loaded into the craft, Charlie brought it to life with the panel's controls.

Starr leaned away from the copilot door as it came down and secured them inside the shuttle. "Can't you let it fly in auto this time?"

Raakor chuckled from the back.

"*Krafka,*" Charlie argued, "when have I ever put anything in auto except for cruising?" The real problem for Starr, even though she'd spent most of her life in outer space, was that flight went against her nature. Starr's feet were bred for solid ground, and the shuttle's lift from the bay floor was a reminder of her jitters.

The shuttle reversed out of the bay with the spaceship's automated assistance. Once clear of the bay, the *Pacifica's* bi-door started sealing back up. The craft continued reversing farther from the ship to gain more clearance, then it banked to the left and headed for Kander.

At the helm, Charlie switched on the communications system and searched for a specific channel. "*Not sure they monitor a frequency,*" she muttered in Jero but then made an attempt and hailed in Kalmarese. "Kander, Kander, this is the shuttle *Pacifica*. Our estimated time of arrival is twenty minutes," she reported over the frequency. A long silence followed, and Charlie prepared to switch off the communication system, but a static sound gave her pause.

"Shuttle *Pacifica*, this is Kander. You are cleared to enter Tarrak's airspacc. I am sending you the exact coordinates for landing."

Charlie exchanged a look with Starr before she replied, "Roger that, Kander." She hesitated because she was unsure if the Kalmar on the other end even understood Earth aviation lingo. She shrugged and said, "We will call back when we enter Tarrak's airspace." She released the mic switch and watched the landing coordinates pull up on the control panel. "Damn. I guess they beefed up air and space security." For the most part, the Kalmar stayed grounded on their planet and took little interest in air or space travel.

Charlie sighed at Starr's quiet demeanor, but the flare-up and the meeting were wreaking havoc on Starr. She refocused on the trip to the planet and increased the throttle. She hated being late. Starr began shaking her right leg, and her nervous energy multiplied as they grew closer to the planet. With an eye roll, Charlie reached to the panel and opened her favorite music list.

Starr glanced at the list and growled when Charlie picked one. "Char—" She was cut off by the sudden noise in the cockpit.

Charlie felt better now that she could ignore Starr's negativity. She wiggled in the pilot's seat and tilted the nose down, the music burning in her blood. While she sang the lyrics, she tapped on the panel and locked on the coordinates to Tarrak.

Starr groaned and glared out the side window.

Early on in their relationship, Starr often turned off the music in the *Pacifica*'s cockpit, commencing a war every time. Charlie would get mad and argue with Starr until one of them demanded that Raakor pick a side. He always declined to be pulled into their ridiculous fight. In the end, Charlie would restart the music but blast it through every speaker in the entire spaceship.

Once in the city's airspace, Charlie radioed ahead that they were only three minutes away from landing at the specified location, then focused on the last of the flight. She enjoyed traveling in outer space, but she loved flying in a planet's atmosphere. Landings required specific skills, and the more difficult the landing site, the better. "The louder the music, the better the landing," Charlie murmured and hummed.

Starr glared at her singing boss but made no effort to shut off the music.

"Whatever it takes," Charlie sang out the title and pointed at Starr, who glowered at her. Charlie placed her other hand on the stick when the shuttle entered half a march above the landing spot. She flipped a few switches and decreased the throttle, all while singing or humming. Their angle toward the ground ate away the distance until the landing point was visible to Charlie.

Starr leaned to the side and peered out the door's window, fidgeting with her lectra gun.

With expert skill, Charlie navigated the craft to the landing spot and allowed it to sink, then hover over the spot. After a few more taps on the control panel, she lowered the shuttle to the grass and started the shutdown process. In the past, Starr would jump out once on solid ground, but this time she unbuckled and sat there until Charlie was done.

"Ready?" Charlie looked at her two crewmen. They were as prepared as possible, especially with the native tongue of Kander.

Starr sighed and muttered, "*Joh*." But she tapped the door's control and climbed out when it started to open. Like Charlie, she had a difficult childhood tied to the planet.

Raakor, who sat behind Charlie, also activated his door and stepped out.

Charlie shook her head at Starr's attitude. She exited the vessel too and smiled at the stern features of the four Kalmar guards, assuming the others were near Starr. Their laser rifles were noteworthy and new technology, at least to the planet. "We're here to see the High Commander," she declared in Kalmarese. Even after years of being away from the planet, the language remained with her as if it'd been packed away in a dusty corner of her mind. The four soldiers were silent and still, other than their breathing, which confirmed they weren't statues, at least. It was a hell of a welcoming party to such a beautiful planet.

Damn these Kalmar, Charlie cursed. She had expected them to at least be surprised by her ability to speak Kalmarese.

"They not in charge," Starr said in a soft voice.

Charlie glanced across the shuttle's roof at Starr's similar situation. Starr's guards were motionless except for one, who had a slight curl to his lip. The guards were aware of Starr's hybrid background after a single sniff. One guard was having a hard time hiding his displeasure.

"But I am," a strong, thick voice announced.

Charlie cut her attention to the Kalmar, who had stepped through the guards. She straightened herself in hopes to gain an inch of height against the Kalmar's taller stance. It was pointless, as the Kalmar towered over her.

"I am Commander Gaveston." For a moment, he stood in front of the foreigners who had been called to his planet. He had a shaven head and broad shoulders, and he wore tattered clothes, including a jacket. Behind his back, a sword's hilt protruded next to his head, but his main weapon was the laser handgun tied to his hip. His tattooed forehead wrinkled when he studied the visitors.

Charlie took one step closer to Gaveston, who was an Alpha among his people. She received the offered arm and shook. "I'm Charlie, and this is Raakor." She indicated to her left, then signaled Starr, who joined her side to protect her. "And this is Starr." She ignored his scowl toward Starr. "We're here to meet with the High Commander."

"I'm well aware," Gaveston stated. A low rumble shook in his chest when he turned his attention to Starr next. He raked his gaze over the despised hybrid, but he faked a neutral expression. "Follow me."

The mercenary team was guided through the field, and the eight guards shadowed them. Several yards from them were two hover trucks, and Gaveston indicated for them to get into one. Once seated on the truck bed's bench, two guards joined them. All the other guards loaded into the second truck.

The quiet ride to the city's entrance took fifteen minutes. The landscape was changing as autumn approached the planet. Charlie enjoyed the chance to soak in the blue sky, bright sun and weaker secondary sun, and one of the two lit moons in the daylight. The city's neighboring fields had new grain, and a few farms had cattle. With a frown, Charlie reminisced about her lost planet and her past that she'd hidden away in her memory when she went to space. Her nostalgia died when the capital city of Tarrak's dark stone face filled her view. A shiver raced down her back, and she looked over at her team.

Starr seemed stoic, but most likely her stomach was a mess. Unlike Charlie, she expressed hating the damn planet more than anything. As they passed the open ancient gates, she sniffed the city's air, which carried probably hundreds of scents such as motor oil, horses, food, and fucking Alphas.

Raakor, for his part, appeared indifferent and studied the changing landscape.

After turning through the streets, the trucks arrived at a gated stone building that was round and at least fifty floors high. The structure had a Greco-Roman feel to it, yet it had been modernized at some point. Its paler stones contrasted against the city's dark stone structures, giving it a godly appeal. So far, it was the only building in the city that had a small lawn and trees around it. Charlie recalled that the Kalmar named it the Great Tower. One by one, everybody filed out of the trucks and followed Gaveston to the main entrance of the Great

Tower. He ordered several guards to stand post and only two remained with them.

Charlie paused at the threshold of the entrance to the Great Tower and gathered her resolve. She moved forward and passed the open wooden doors into the one place that few humans entered.

The main entrance opened into a grand foyer with a soaring ceiling that went nearly to the top of the building, but they had no time for a tour. Commander Gaveston bore left and guided the mercenary team to the steps that spiraled up the entire fifty or so floors of the building—if one was interested in walking them all. At the second floor, they stepped off the landing and went into a small, bare room. An elevator opened and allowed them to go up to the very top.

With a glance at the number of floors on the touchscreen, Charlie realized that there were fifty-three floors to be precise. The Kalmar race was superstitious, and fifty-three was revered as a lucky number. Upon coming out of the lift, they stepped out onto the highest floor in the tower, which was the throne room reserved for the High Commander.

To the left were two grand, sealed wooden doors to the throne room. The guard on either side straightened when Commander Gaveston neared them. Each one held a spear in their hand, more for display than purpose.

Gaveston faced Charlie, who grew tense and mirrored both Starr and Raakor's stances. They were surrounded by guards whose Alpha scents had to be bombarding Starr. Hearing a familiar grumble, she prayed Starr could keep it together rather than let the damn flare-up control her.

Gaveston looked at Charlie, as if the rest of the team were ghosts. "You are to address the High Commander as Kal. And you must leave all weapons with the guards."

Charlie reached for her handgun. She sensed Starr's questioning gaze, so she nodded at her crewmembers to follow the orders.

Starr couldn't help making another displeased noise but unhooked her first weapon and glared at the guard who approached them.

Charlie handed the gun to Gaveston, then jerked her sheathed blade free from under her jacket. She relinquished it next. She swore if anything happened to her weapons, she was going to twist Gaveston into a pretzel.

"These will be returned to you once you depart Tarrak." Gaveston handed the weapons to the guard on his right. He ignored the perturbed looks and went to the doors that were opened for him and the others.

Raakor was the last to hand over his two handguns and a small dagger, grumbling when the guard took it. Meanwhile Starr blew out a deep breath and raised an eyebrow at Charlie, who shrugged in reply.

Charlie followed behind Gaveston, whose large build blocked most of the view in front of her. The throne room was massive, causing the mass of people to seem smaller than they were. Like the Great Tower, it was round and had a beautiful white marble floor with gray and yellow veins snaking through it. Overhead, the ceiling was made from stained glass that depicted the birth of the planet's main god, Kalatas. Each color from the decorative glass poured down over the floor, lighting the way to the dais.

All around the room were numerous Kalmar of high rank. Starr's low growl confirmed they were Alphas, and even Charlie was frazzled by it. She didn't want to be in Starr's skin, having such an acute sense of smell. However, her confidence grew further with Starr and Raakor flanking her from behind.

Commander Gaveston stepped off to his right and departed from the group. He left them in the center of the large round throne room and stood by another Alpha dressed in warrior attire.

Charlie pulled her attention away from the line of Alpha faces and looked straight ahead at the Kalmar throne. Before her was a grand yet natural display of an old throne set upon a marble dais. The chiseled, pale throne rose from the white dais and had thick black veins shooting up from the base and to the arm rests. The back of the throne was adorned with tree branches that twisted and spiraled upward until they met at one point. The throne's top had a small flat wood shelf that was large enough to hold an object or two.

However, it wasn't the throne that captivated Charlie but the High Commander, who filled the throne with power and mystery. The ruler sat proud and rigid, dark clothes contrasted against the throne's sharp white. Bright green eyes conveyed something both ancient and dark within them. A god sat among mere mortals.

As Charlie absorbed every detail of the High Commander, she swallowed hard at the most unusual feature about the ruler. The High Commander was indeed an Alpha, every pulse of aggressive energy proved it. However, the High Commander's chest swelled with breasts, their features were soft and feminine save for a small scar, and their wavy black hair flowed behind broad shoulders.

This Alpha was a different kind and looked like a female human. For a beat, Charlie thumbed through all her education about Kalmar, yet nothing came to mind that Alphas were ever females. Or rather, Alphas that looked like Omegas but were still Alphas… or something. Charlie was at a loss. But she was certain Kal was a *she*.

"You are late."

Charlie lifted her chin and pursed her lips at the truthful remark. Fuck, she hated being late, and the damn High Commander had to point it out in public. "Our apologies." She cleared her throat after her voice came out hoarse. "Kal." She frowned when Kal's eyes cut from her to Raakor and then settled on Starr, narrowing more.

Starr shook with a low rumble, yet Charlie caught it. She prayed nobody else heard it, especially the High Commander, or they may have a fight on their hands.

"But we are here now, as requested," Charlie continued. Her stomach fluttered when those bright green eyes returned to her, and she chided herself for reacting to it.

"It would seem so." Kal canted her head, as if assessing something about Charlie. Her deep stare might undo Charlie if their strange game didn't end.

With better confidence, Charlie focused on why they came here and said, "Your message mentioned a kidnapping." Her prompt broke the spell between them. She was able to breathe when Kal spoke.

"*Ja*," Kal agreed. "About three days ago, a Kalmar citizen was kidnapped and taken by two male humans and one female human."

Charlie hummed low and narrowed her eyes at the mention of humans but asked, "And you need us to recover the citizen?"

After a slight nod, Kal remained quiet, and a curious note was in her features before it was gone. "The citizen was taken off-world from Kander, beyond our reach."

Charlie better understood the issue and why they were asked to come to Kander. Kalmar hated outer space. "Have they contacted anybody since then?"

"*Ja*, they contacted the family and have made demands for the safe return of the Omega."

"What was the ransom?" Charlie asked. Few people came to Kander, and to kidnap a citizen seemed rather purposeful. However, the drawn-out silence made Charlie wonder if she'd have an answer. The information wasn't pertinent to their rescue mission, but Charlie was nosy.

"Ten loads of darakar." Kal's voice thundered through the silent room. The timber and depth of her voice threaded through Charlie's being.

Charlie closed her eyes and opened them after a deep breath, struggling to focus on the conversation rather than letting the ruler's voice affect her. She blinked once after her mind jumped to the special, rare fuel that was located on Kander and no other planet in the galaxy. Darakar was known for burning at a slow rate on ships. The fuel was worth millions or even billions of stills out on the galaxy's market. Of course, the outer space–hating Kalmar were the ones sitting on it.

"You were recommended to us," Kal said. Charlie had thought Kal was ignoring Raakor and Starr, as Commander Gaveston and the other Alphas had, but then Kal shifted her attention to the rest of the mercenary team. "You all were."

Starr replied with a soft huff, which went unheard due to the grumbles throughout the throne room from the audience. The people's displeasure with Kal's acknowledgment of Starr was expected, but it improved her opinion of the ruler.

"We want you to return the citizen to us, alive and unharmed."

Charlie nodded at Kal's request. "And the kidnappers?" She fought off swooning when the stoic ruler flashed a wolfish smile. She needed to get a grip and focus on the pending negotiation for the job.

"Bring them to me. Alive."

Needing a beat, Charlie regained control of her hormones or whatever the hell was wrong with her. After a measured breath, she raised an eyebrow and got down to business. "How many stills?"

"Two hundred thousand for the Omega's return."

Charlie nibbled on her lip and did some math in her head. She was good with numbers, similar to learning different languages. Holding back a grin, she argued, "Three hundred thousand stills for the Omega's return and a hundred thousand stills for each kidnapper we bring back." She clenched her jaw when Kal's eyes went from a vibrant green to a dangerous gray. Then tensions rose further when a robed, bald Alpha peeled himself off the wall and started approaching Charlie.

Charlie's team reacted, but she calmed them down with a sharp order.

Kal flicked her right hand, which halted the robed Alpha's attempt to reprimand Charlie. After the Alpha returned to his spot, Kal rumbled and spoke with a soft growl. "One hundred thousand stills for the Omega and fifty thousand stills for each kidnapper."

Charlie placed her hands on her hips and lowered her gaze to the floor. She could think clearer when the damn High Commander's eyes weren't drilling into her very soul. After thinking, her gaze raked over Kal until she met Kal's piercing stare. "A hundred thousand stills for the Omega isn't even worth us starting our ship's engines."

Kal's lips pulled back a little with each word from Charlie, and her fingers curled into the chair's armrest. A strange but dangerous energy hummed around her and spilled down from the throne.

"Two hundred thousand stills for the Omega and fifty thousand stills per kidnapper." Charlie was placing the bulk of the stills on the Omega's life, the more important and constant part. Nobody had an idea whether or not the kidnappers were three goons or part of a larger organization. It was probable that the kidnappers had a boss.

As the quietness grew, so did the thick tension, and it caused beads of sweat to form on Charlie's brow. To her side, a soft hiss from Starr worried her further. If this damn deal fell through, then they were back in the ship with half a tank of fuel, stills wasted to get here, and no new job. If she could win this job, it would make them well-known; they would be the first mercenaries to ever be hired by the Kalmar.

With clenched hands, Charlie went in for the last attempt to score the job. "You're not going to find many mercenaries who handle kidnappings." She held Kal's gaze, never breaking the contact. "And I don't think you're willing to risk an Omega."

Kal's low rumble thundered through the throne room. She appeared calm, but the darkness in her eyes reflected her ire. Toward Charlie or the idea of the Omega being harmed, Charlie was unsure. Perhaps a bit of both. But Kal raised her chin and said, "Final offer is two hundred thousand stills for the Omega. Thirty thousand stills for each kidnapper brought back alive and fifteen thousand for a head." Every word dripped with a finality, and her curled lips started to reveal her distinct canines.

Charlie struggled with her breathing, and her heart slammed against her chest. She tried thinking over the deal, even though her mind was foggy from the edgy bartering. It was clear that Kal was done with their game, and she had to take whatever was offered or lose out. After clearing her throat, she bought more time and asked, "Mind if I confer with my crew quickly?"

Kal narrowed her eyes but indicated her team with a single flick of her finger.

Charlie flashed a smile at Kal, then smirked at the curious glint in Kal's stony features. She spun on her boot heels and switched to speaking in Jero, knowing the Kalmar couldn't understand it. "*What do you think?*"

Starr gave a displeased sound but replied, "*We should take the deal.*" She looked to Raakor for his opinion, wondering if he was going to agree with Starr. He shifted his attention from the High Commander to Charlie and gave a faint nod. "*Yes,*" he agreed in Jero.

"*There is something else going on though,*" Charlie said. There was more to the kidnapped Omega, who was important, very important, if she was worth two hundred thousand stills.

"*Yes,*" Starr agreed, then narrowed her eyes and said, "*but it doesn't matter.*"

After a deep breath, Charlie felt focused again, and the conversation helped her see the goal at hand.

"*Take the deal, Charlie.*"

Charlie gave a thin smile at Raakor's urgent words. She turned back to Kal and noticed how the crowd went quiet after whispering among themselves. She grinned at Kal, who perhaps had been curious about the strange language. "We agree to the deal."

An uproar started in the throne room, either in displeasure or frustration, that their High Commander had hired an Earthling, a Hurr, and a degenerate hybrid. But the Kalmar had few to no options due to their lack of interest in space travel. The Kalmar were at their mercy if they wanted the Omega returned to the planet.

"It is done," Kal announced. Her heavy voice carried through the throne room and silenced her people. She then signaled Gaveston and said, "We will discuss the details later, but until then, you will stay as guests."

"We prefer to get to work," Charlie argued, but Kal's darkened features made her shoulders tighten in reaction.

"It was not a request."

Gaveston approached, and the guards came up behind them.

Charlie narrowed her eyes at feeling more like a prisoner than a guest. Sharp words sat on the tip of her tongue, but she snapped her jaw shut before it was too late.

"Show them each to their rooms, Commander," Kal ordered.

"*Ja*, Kal."

Charlie itched for her handgun and noticed Starr fingering empty air where the handgun would have rested on her hip. *Damn Alphas and their control issues*, she seethed. She reined in on her frustration and took the lead before her crew had a chance to react.

Together, they followed the guards and Gaveston out of the throne room. As soon as the double doors were closed, voices boomed from behind them, but Charlie ignored it. Looking to her team, she switched to the Jero language. "*That went well.*"

"*Exceptional,*" Raakor agreed in a monotone voice.

Starr huffed and continued toward the elevators. "*We got what we wanted.*"

"*Not quite yet,*" Charlie muttered. They still had a mission to complete before they could collect any stills. She looked over at Gaveston, who held the elevator for them. As she stepped past him, a chill raced down her back and left prickles on her skin. A low rumble filled the small space between them, but she sensed Starr's front pressing into her back.

Gaveston's eyes lifted to Starr, who was protecting Charlie.

As the two faced off, Charlie choked on the battle of dominance between them. She tugged on Starr's jacket to get her into the elevator. She was thankful that Raakor was a Hurr and had no high sense of smell or need to dominate. Starr was reluctant at first but gave into the command and entered the elevator along with the two guards.

Charlie focused on Gaveston, who seemed amused by Starr's subordinate nature toward a human. For a moment, Charlie hung on a mental edge of being snide with Gaveston but knew it would only make things worse. With a deep breath, she spoke in a dangerous tone. "Starr isn't the real threat, but I can be." Smirking at his annoyed look, she winked at him and entered the elevator next to her team.

After a grunt, Gaveston shut the elevator gate with more force than necessary, then stepped back once. He folded his arms and remained silent during the ride down; however, his overbearing Alpha scent filled the confines.

After reaching their designated floor, they exited the cramped elevator and followed Gaveston down a long hallway filled with sealed rooms, one after another, like a hotel. The assigned rooms were rather comfortable, but their supplies were on the ship, and they had nothing with them.

Chapter 3

"H*ey, Raakor.*"

Raakor filled the doorway to his assigned room and stepped out. "*What's going on, boss?*"

"*We're meeting in Starr's room,*" Charlie explained in Jero, then followed him to the next door and knocked on it. As they waited, the guards eyed them, but nobody spoke. Starr appeared relieved when she saw Charlie and Raakor on the other side and closed the door after they came into her room.

"*How are you holding up?*"

Starr shrugged at Charlie's question and went to the sofa in front of the fireplace. "*The meds are helping.*"

Raakor neared the fireplace and stood next to it, arms folded against his chest.

Charlie sunk into the empty spot beside Starr and noticed the uneaten food on the coffee table in front of them. She had eaten the meal that the guard brought her, but Starr hadn't had hers. The flare-up limited her appetite for at least three days.

"*Have you heard anything?*" Starr asked the pair.

After holding up a finger at her crew, Charlie dug out her techbit and tapped on it a few times. A soft pulse went through the room as an invisible sound barrier swept twenty feet around them. The techbit emitted a hum while it blocked all noise from leaving the field. They might be speaking in Jero, but she didn't want to take an unnecessary chance.

After putting the techbit on the table, Charlie looked at her team. "*I haven't spoken to anyone. Not sure what is going on here.*" She watched the strained lines on Starr's features and prayed that the flare-up would be faster than normal.

"*Do you think we'll be here long?*" Raakor asked.

With a headshake, Charlie murmured, "*I don't know.*" She picked up the techbit again and pulled up the connection to the *Pacifica.*

Starr shifted on the sofa and wiped her damp brow. "*How do things look back on the ship?*"

"*Everything seems fine,*" Charlie replied. They wouldn't have to worry about anybody bothering their ship since it was rare for Kander to receive visitors. There were a few merchant ships that flew to Kander and sold their wares. Otherwise, there wasn't much traffic coming to the planet.

"*We don't have any supplies or clothes,*" Raakor reminded.

Charlie shut off the techbit's screen and returned it to the table. "*Maybe I can convince the High Commander to let us go up to the ship.*"

"*We need more weapons than just our handguns,*" Starr mentioned.

A few times Charlie's head moved in agreement before her mind drifted back to today's meeting. "*We won't be here that long. They need that Omega back.*" She looked at Starr. "*That Omega is important to somebody.*"

After a grunt, Starr said, "*She's important to our stills account.*"

Sighing, Charlie knew the flare-up was hindering Starr's capacity for reasoning, even if the medication quelled most of her natural urges. Regardless of Starr's trouble, her presence during the mission was important and would always benefit them.

"*It is peculiar,*" Raakor agreed. "*The Omega must be valuable to somebody.*"

"*It's possible that they give damn about all their citizens,*" Starr argued, her voice heavy with frustration. "*Their High Commander is a god and is known for caring about all Kalmar.*"

Charlie sighed and put aside her curious concerns on the topic until something else came to mind. "*Did you know the High Commander was… Omega-ish?*" She huffed at Starr's low laugh.

"*The High Commander is an Alpha.*"

Grumbling, Charlie argued, "*But she has feminine features.*" She shook her head and muttered, "*A female Alpha.*" She was rather knowledgeable about Kalmar, if not more so than Starr. However, a female Alpha, or whatever they were called, was new to Charlie.

"*Perhaps she's an unusual breed of Alpha,*" Raakor suggested and shrugged at them.

With a low hum, Charlie considered the idea and then asked, "*Are there male Omegas?*"

Starr held out her hands and shook her head. "*I'm not sure. I left this damn forsaken planet when I was six.*"

Starr had left Kander at an early age, escaping death from the Degenerate Kill Order that was put into effect by the last High Commander. From conception, Starr was cursed by both Kalmar and Earthlings because her Alpha father and human mother had fallen for each other. Starr hinted at her past life on Kander but refrained from telling many stories about her childhood.

Pursing her lips, Charlie weighed the High Commander's unusual attributes as both an Alpha and an Omega. The High Commander was as large as any Alpha, was aggressive, and seemed to give off an Alpha scent. However, the High Commander had soft features and breasts like an Omega, along with self-control that wasn't normal for an Alpha. After a heavy sigh, she joked, "*She's like an Alphega or something.*"

Starr grunted, leaned into Charlie's space, and whispered, "*Maybe you should ask her what's between her legs to confirm which one she really is.*" She earned a hard smack to her bicep, and she laughed at Charlie's reaction.

"*Shut up,*" Charlie retorted.

Raakor rolled his eyes and straightened from leaning against the mantle. "*What's the plan now?*"

"*Maybe we'll be out of here tomorrow,*" Charlie offered and glanced at the techbit, which denoted the local time as nearly eight o'clock in the evening. The planet took twenty-six hours to complete a full rotation, unlike former Earth's twenty-four hours. Sometimes it was a real pain in the ass to spend any length of time on another planet that had different measurements. At an early age, Charlie realized that time was an invention and that outer space's concept of time was mysterious to all beings, maybe even to the gods.

"*Let's hope,*" Starr muttered and rubbed her damp forehead.

Charlie had a soft frown and studied her friend with concern. One benefit to staying on Kander was it gave Starr more time to work through her flare-up before they started the mission. They would be in luck if it at least tapered off before they left Kander.

Charlie reached over and squeezed Starr's knee. "Is there anything I can do?" Starr's adamant headshake said it all. Once early on in their relationship, Charlie had offered sex to help subdue the flare-up, but she had been rejected.

Starr would always reject her.

* * *

At dawn, the light streamed through the sliver of an opening in the drapes and crept up Charlie's soft features. She was half buried under the blankets in her private room. The night had been a little chilly due to the early autumn weather. Kalmar homes and buildings were warmed by a combination of fireplaces and geothermal heating. On the *Pacifica*, her quarters never saw natural light due to the lack of windows. The warmth of the sunlight was a welcomed change. She stretched before going for a shower.

The bathroom was large enough for two people to be comfortable. Everything was made from beautiful white stone. Nothing like the plastics on Earth. The Kalmar were people of nature and were kind to their planet. Whatever they harvested from the planet, they tried to reuse and replace rather than waste. Even their clothing was worn, re-worn, and patched until the threads all but disintegrated on their bodies. It was the Kalmar's conservation efforts that held back the overconsumption of the planet's darakar. There were various rumors that the Kalmar horded their own darakar. But at limited times, it was sold on the galaxy's market to obtain stills. Charlie suspected the stills were then used to make improvements on the planet's minor technology.

One small blessing on Kander was the electricity, but it was minimal. Every drop of electricity derived from solar, wind, or water rather than from sources that polluted Kander. Charlie admired the Kalmar for their clean energy. After the refreshing shower, she dressed and tied her boots, until knocking on the door grabbed her attention. Starr was often the first one to start their days.

However, after opening the door, Charlie frowned at the visitor on the other side.

Commander Gaveston stood proud, as usual. Behind him were the two guards. He returned Charlie's glower and stated, "Kal has requested your presence."

Charlie's features tightened further. What could the High Commander need at this hour? She wanted to bring her team.

"Now," Gaveston snapped.

"Let me get my crew." Charlie stepped out but was halted by Gaveston in her path. She fisted her hands and pinned him with a dark glare. Gaveston was a typical Alpha knothead. At least the damn High Commander was tolerable. Perhaps Kal's feminine qualities played into her more sensible personality.

"Only you. Not your crew," Gaveston stated with disgust in his tone. He wreaked of a harsh spice that made Charlie want to recoil.

Charlie narrowed her eyes. Gaveston would carry out the order with any means, even if it meant tossing Charlie over his shoulder. There were few options for her. She decided on the easy route and nodded at him. "Lead the way."

Gaveston marched off, followed by Charlie, and then one of the guards. The journey through the tall building didn't take long. After a short elevator trip up, they arrived at a set of sealed doors that were left unguarded. Gaveston pointed at it.

Charlie huffed at him. In the past, she had heard about Alphas and seen them at a distance. There were plenty of stories about their volatile nature. Gaveston was her first true interaction with one. As a human, she was seen as lesser, but she didn't play into the weak role of humans. Outer space and life as a mercenary had taught her how to handle many different personalities, species, and races. There was no superior race in the galaxy. But as she focused on the door, she realized there were certain individuals in this galaxy who were more than mere mortals. The High Commander was a god in flesh and an Alpha of all the Alphas.

With a sigh, she pushed open the door. Straight ahead was a desk and in front of it was the High Commander, whose presence filled the entire space. Charlie paused in the doorway, but a harsh shove from Gaveston sent her stumbling forward. She flashed a weak smile at the enraged ruler. However, the anger wasn't directed at her but at the poor sap under Kal's boot.

"Failure is not acceptable." Kal snarled at the fallen Alpha soldier under her heel. She continued applying pressure to his throat, almost about to crush it if he didn't heed to her.

"*Ja*, Kal," the soldier agreed and gasped. He clawed at the stone floor under him, his face squashed into it. Drops of blood were beside his face on the marble.

Kal's dark eyes flickered to Charlie, then she chuffed and ordered, "Report back with better news in two days."

The soldier scrambled to his feet and touched his throat. He gulped before saying, "*Ja*, Kal." He bowed out of the room before he lost any more pride.

Charlie fought a nervous laugh after seeing a show of power. The awkward situation left her both uneasy and a bit turned on. She tried to shake off her body's natural reaction to Kal's strong presence. After releasing a shaky breath, she jumped when Kal spoke to her.

"We have much to discuss this morning."

Charlie cleared her throat, as if feeling the boot choking herself. She tried ignoring why Kal's raw, dark power excited her. "*Ja*, we do." She became better focused and stated, "I would prefer if my crew were here."

Kal stepped behind a long wooden desk and picked up a foldable tech tablet that leaned against the window, most likely solar charging. "Why?" She approached Charlie and added, "You are in charge."

Charlie parted her lips and yet gave pause at Kal's insightfulness. A long time ago, she had been told several times that Alphas had an intellect of a rock. The heart and soul of the Kalmar race were in the Omegas. "Because we're a damn team."

After a low rumble, Kal's lips curled into a wolfish smile. "The hybrid is in heat and therefore cannot think clearly, much less provide any useful element to this meeting." She tilted her head and added, "And the Hurr will not speak."

With a downturn of her lips, Charlie stared up into eyes that were as bright as the planet, glowing like green fire. There were countless myths that the High Commanders held the very spirit of the Kalmar's god in them. For a heartbeat, she was lost in those green orbs, looking for answers to her own soul. But she blinked away the trance when Kal shifted to Charlie's side.

"You speak our language well," Kal remarked.

"For a human," Charlie quipped. A low, thick rumble sounded at her back, and she grew tenser when

Kal stood behind her. She suspected Kal was a foot and a half taller, if not more. Charlie had always had a weak spot for someone taller than her.

Kal lowered her head closer to Charlie, into her personal space. "Our language does not travel to outer space," she whispered. "And I highly doubt the hybrid taught you so quickly." After a huff, she stated, "You have a distinct dialect to your Kalmarese."

"So do you," Charlie remarked without thought. She stiffened after voicing her observation, but it had occurred to her after interacting with Gaveston several times. He drew out certain vowel-like sounds, whereas Kal spoke like Charlie and Starr. It was possible Kal was from the same province or general area as Charlie and Starr. However, Charlie wasn't here to discuss her past and deflected before it was too late. "I'm from Earth."

"Many humans are from Earth." Kal took one step closer to Charlie's left side. She gave a predatory smile, revealing her sharp canines, and went in for the kill. "Dorlon."

Charlie almost choked on her tongue after hearing an old but familiar name. She jerked her attention to the face so close to hers. "How did you…?" The pieces now clicked together on how she and her crew were selected among all the galaxy mercenaries. Dorlon's adorable childhood features drifted through her mind. A dull ache entered her heart. Dorlon wasn't the only person Charlie had left behind.

Raine, Charlie's memory whispered to her. But she pushed away the happy laughs from their three-person squad. Those days were gone.

"Dorlon was my mentor," Kal replied. "She also recommended you for this job."

Charlie shook her head against the old childhood memories. She had stored her past deep in the recesses of her mind until Kal unlocked it with one name. Needing space, she moved away and whispered, "She was one of my best friends." And Charlie's first romantic crush.

Kal stared, reaching into Charlie's soul and reading every hidden note in her heart. "She said you saved her life."

Charlie snorted, folded her arms and stared into her past. "She was fishing on a rock in the same river, the one that bordered our villages. I showed up a little later, scared her, and she fell into the rushing water." She regarded Kal again. "Your people hate water, and she couldn't swim. I jumped in and got her to shore."

Kal narrowed her eyes and remained quiet.

Charlie shook her head. "She was so pissed that she slapped mud onto my face." She grinned when Kal gave an amused grunt. "One year later to the day, she finally thanked me for saving her." She shrugged and muttered, "Even though it was my fault."

With calmer features, Kal neared Charlie. "She feels you will handle the situation carefully."

Charlie tucked away her memories and focused on the task at hand. She nodded. "I will," she assured.

After a low rumble, Kal stated, "Good, because Dorlon staked her reputation on you." She went to the sitting area that had a fireplace. "Join me." There was a three-person sofa and two wing chairs and a wooden table in the middle.

Charlie was bothered by Dorlon's choice. Honored, yes, but worried nonetheless. From Kal's position in the middle of the couch, they would be seated close together. Had Kal done it on purpose? With an inward groan, she settled into the sofa and did her best to act natural.

Kal retrieved a folded tablet from her overcoat, bringing it out of its sleep mode. Once the device was unfolded to its full size, she tapped its screen until a photo appeared. "These are the pictures of the kidnappers' ship."

Charlie was forced to lean into the ruler's space so she could have a better view. Nothing was familiar about the ship, and there were no affiliation markings on it. She frowned at the lack of information. The only thing that stood out was the ship's old, bulky nature, which indicated that it was a transporter.

After a moment, Kal flipped to the next image, which was a close-up of the cockpit of the ship. She could see the outline of two faces in the front seats and that was all. The details were blurry even with the ship's reflective glass helping to offset the solar flare.

"Can I see?"

Charlie accepted the oversized tablet. It made her realize how much larger built Alphas were compared to humans. She focused on the pictures, swiped between them, and zoomed in and out to search for additional details. Any clue could help them locate the kidnappers, who could be anyone in the huge galaxy. After a headshake, Charlie said, "I need a copy of these images." She had contacts she could reach out to, to locate the ship's owner. She reached into her leather jacket pocket for her techbit.

"*Joh*," Kal denied.

Charlie paused and looked up from the tablet to Kal's stern features. "It's a lead," she argued, but a shudder passed through her when Kal flashed a dark smile.

"I already have a plan in motion. It is why you are still here."

Charlie returned the techbit to its home inside her jacket, then narrowed her eyes. "What plan?" She hated being caught off guard.

"The kidnappers demanded ten shipments of darakar. When we give them the final one, they will return the Omega to us." Kal paused and tilted her head. "I have already responded to their demands. The kidnappers will send word when they want to collect the first shipment of darakar."

"What?" Charlie was wide-eyed and fumbled with the tablet but didn't drop it. "Don't you think you should have discussed this with me before making that call?" More heat entered her voice with each word.

Kal matched the anger with a threatening snarl. "It was my decision to make. You work for me."

Charlie straightened and realized her strength paled to Kal's own, which became a thick veil of dark power that washed over Charlie. Her ire was extinguished. The strange power tried to strangle the fight out of

Charlie, except she held her position a little longer. Kal's raw influence crawled off, allowing her to breathe fresh air.

Kal popped up, stomped away, and snarled low before she said, "When the kidnappers arrive to collect the darakar, they will be killed. Then you and your team will assume their places."

"Killed?" Charlie scowled in Kal's direction and an edge entered her tone. "Our agreement is that we're paid fifteen a head. But now one, two, or all of them will be killed by you?" Red-hot heat started pulsing through her veins. She clenched the sofa in an effort to stay in control rather than get in the High Commander's face.

"You should have considered that detail before agreeing."

Charlie launched out of the sofa and matched Kal's aggressive stance. If this was a battle of wills, she was the most willful being in this whole damn galaxy, mortal or otherwise. She was nearing a dangerous outburst, except for the fact that she was in the middle of the Kalmar capital, in the Great Tower, in the room with the highest power, and weaponless. She took a measured breath, then leaned into Kal's personal space.

Kal rumbled and revealed her canines, granting Charlie a low sneer.

Charlie ignored the threat and spoke in a calm tone while her fists shook at her side. "Trick me again, and I won't return your Omega." A cruel smile came over her. "Instead I'll sell her to the highest bidder for more stills." She was undeterred by Kal's threatening growl. "I swear it."

Towering over Charlie, Kal was immense and strong, more than capable of cutting Charlie down. Any Alpha would do so, in Charlie's mind. Her scent was hot and spicy, similar to Gaveston's Alpha smell, but far more pleasant even during an argument. In truth, Charlie found Kal's scent attractive and struggled against its draw. As the heartbeats passed, she expected Kal to unleash on her. But to her amazement, Kal composed herself and showed her rare ability to have self-control over her inner Alpha, unlike all the others on Kander. After a deep breath, she spoke in an even tone. "Bring the Omega safely back to me, and I promise the darakar is yours."

"Wait. What?" Charlie was jarred from her challenging stance and dropped her shoulders. Six ingots of the fuel alone could be worth hundreds or even thousands of stills. Once the rush faded away, her mind connected a few dots. "This Omega must mean something to you." Perhaps the Omega was Kal's own, but Charlie hadn't noticed a bite mark on Kal's neck and assumed the ruler was unmated, which was common for many Kals.

"All Kalmar are important to me." Kal spoke with evenness and left nothing to question.

After a sigh, Charlie returned to the sofa and weighed the earlier plan, before the fight. "So the kidnappers come, and we take the ship. That's assuming we can crack their ship's security." It wasn't a horrible plan but not something she would have done.

"I was told your Hurr is skilled with tech." Kal returned to her seat too.

Charlie gave a faint nod. "Most of the time, so let's hope this is one of those times." Even with the pictures, she had no clue what kind of a system was on the ship. She hoped it was one that was easy for Raakor.

Kal eyed Charlie, then picked up the tablet from the low table. "Let us hope, for your sake." She started for the desk.

Fucking Alphas and their control issues, Charlie cursed for the second time. After such an ugly meeting, Charlie was half convinced that Kal had a dick between her legs considering Kal's mile-long dominance streak. She sensed their meeting was over, sooner than planned, but she was fine with it. She needed space from the overbearing, cocky Alpha. However, her stubborn nature to have the last word spurred her onward, and she looked over at Kal.

"If we're staying on the ground this long, we need our things from our ship and for the job." Charlie was grateful they were calmer. They sat with their thighs close and knees grazing side by side. She preferred to keep people out of her personal space unless she was having sex. Somehow Kal's closeness wasn't uncomfortable.

After a moment of consideration, Kal nodded and said, "One of your crewmen may return to your ship today." When Charlie glared, Kal smirked and added, "You will remain here."

Charlie took two deep breaths and held back the bite in her next question. "And these damn guards?" She wondered how much distrust flowed in Kal's veins. She expected a hot reaction, welcoming it. Instead, Kal showed indifference.

"The guards are not for our protection but yours." Kal tilted her head. "Especially your hybrid partner."

Charlie gave pause after hearing why. Kal had also referred to Starr as a hybrid rather than a degenerate. She blew out a breath and accepted their situation.

"You are free to go into the city and explore it."

Charlie weighed the idea because she hated sitting around and waiting for action. Tarrak was new to her and would be interesting to explore. "The Degenerate Kill Order ended years ago."

Kal straightened after the mention of the old order. "*Ja*, but there are those outside of Kander who still pay handsomely for a hybrid. I would hate to see your crewmember subjected to it. We do have space merchants and traders here at times."

Charlie flinched at the truth and ugliness of the outdated bounty on hybrids. At one time the hybrid was thoroughly tortured, including rape, emasculation, castration, or sodomization, before he or she was killed. It was an ugly part of the Kalmar's history that made Charlie sick. As she looked at Kal, she saw a note of sympathy in those green eyes. How could this person be the planet's ruler? The last Kal had honored the bounty, but this one seemed to be against it.

"Commander Gaveston will escort one of your crewmen to the shuttle so you may obtain your supplies," Kal said and departed from the sitting area, ending their meeting.

Charlie went to the office door and considered mentioning Commander Gaveston's extra-large attitude that had to be compensating for a small penis. Instead, she stayed quiet and left the office without another word.

* * *

Charlie sensed the guard on her heels after she stepped off the elevator. She did her best to ignore the shadow while she went down to the main entrance of the Great Tower. As the open front doors came into view, she slowed upon seeing a familiar Alpha coming into the building. It took a tick to place him as the one who attempted to silence her yesterday at the meeting. She clenched her hands in natural defense and became cautious when he gave her a tight smile.

"*Turen*, Charlie," he greeted in a polite tone. "I am Lennox." He wore a black robe, like yesterday, or perhaps it was the same one. He hid his hands in the sleeves until offering his right one.

Charlie tried smiling and clasped his forearm in a solid, firm hold. The thick muscle tightened against her fingers and palm as they held strong, daring the other to break first.

Lennox released first and said, "I am Kal's Head Advisor."

Charlie studied his face, or what she could see of it beyond his neat beard. His facial hair made up for the lack of hair on his shaven, tattooed head. It seemed the tattoo's razor pattern carried up his forehead, across his scalp, and down to the back of his head meant something to him.

"Kal is pleased you have taken the mission to return our citizen to us."

After a low hum, Charlie revealed a smile that was forced. "The stills make it worth it." She refused to be baited into small talk that could bite her later as gossip. It was easier to hide behind a mercenary's greedy mask.

"And the fame," Lennox suggested. Beyond his open posture was a hardness in his brown eyes.

"That can't hurt either." Charlie shifted to the left, about to sidestep him.

"Are you headed into the city?"

Charlie paused and replied, "*Ja.* I've had enough of my room."

Lennox nodded and offered, "I am happy to show you around the city."

After mock consideration, Charlie shook her head and offered a fake smile. "I prefer to wander alone." She then indicated her shadow. "Or as alone as possible."

Lennox bowed his head, an unusual thing for an Alpha to do. "It was nice to meet you."

"You too, Lennox." Charlie passed him and heard a brief exchange between Lennox and the guard. Outside the Great Tower, a beautiful autumn day greeted her. The dual suns warmed her pale skin. The afternoon's blue sky and puffy clouds made Charlie yearn for a simpler life that she'd had as a child until there was nothing but blood and destruction. She shoved the bubbling memories away and focused on the walk into the city streets.

Tarrak was one of the oldest cities on the planet and the heart that pumped life into all the fourteen regions and countless provinces of the Kalmar realm. Every political movement started in Tarrak, every religious miracle and every invention. Tarrak had grown outward from its center from the labor and tears put into it. From Charlie's earlier flight, it was easy to see how the city had sprouted alongside a prominent river, then grew out and away from the Great Tower. The original windy, narrow cobbled streets widened and straightened as the city crept farther toward the east. The first homes near the Great Tower were small, while the ones farther out were taller and wider as wealth and prosperity among the citizens flourished.

But there were scars on the city's face from wars and the most recent battle brought on by the Earthlings' arrival. The humans' own influence on the city had crept into the streets, on the Kalmar's bitter faces, and at the markets. Charlie was surprised to find pieces of tech for sale at the stalls. Much of the tech was dated, but it was still useful on Kander. It wasn't until she came to the far end of the market that she discovered the one person who was monopolizing tech repair.

A human woman with raven hair was seated at a work table and cursing in English at a piece of tech in her hands.

Charlie was drawn closer, observing the familiar woman fight with an old two-way radio.

As if sensing her, the woman met Charlie's gaze and scrambled to grab her falling screwdriver. "Charlie?" she demanded. She placed the device onto the table with all the other tools and equipment. "*Holy fuck*," she whispered in old English.

Charlie was stunned herself and couldn't back away, now that she'd been spotted. "*Hey,* Raine," she greeted back in English. She hoped her English was still good after using Jero for so long.

Raine hurried around the table and exchanged a quick hug with her long-lost friend. "*You're actually alive.*" She admired Charlie before saying, "*Everyone thought…*" She shook her head, then punched Charlie in the arm before switching back to Kalmarese. "Where the *hell* have you been?"

Charlie pointed up to the sky and replied, "Space."

Raine huffed and folded her arms. "Didn't you get enough of that damn place when we came across the galaxy in the *Liberator*?"

Charlie shivered at the name of the starship from her childhood. It was an ugly, oily place whose memory lived in a dark hole of her mind. "Just of the trip here." She trailed her eyes over to the stand and remarked, "Nice business."

Raine's bright grin stood out against her brown skin, and she shrugged before she said, "It's good money." She then nodded at Charlie's interesting dress attire that was a mixture of human and space renegade. "What's your business?"

With a smirk, Charlie replied, "Galaxy mercenary."

Raine laughed and nodded a few times. "Pretty badass." With a sly grin, she teased, "Do they call you Star Lord?"

Rolling her eyes, Charlie said, "Galaxy Master, actually." From Raine's narrowed gaze, she could tell that Raine was unsure whether Charlie was being serious or not. For a moment, she continued taking in her old friend's features, which were aged. She now sported a scar on her left cheek. It seemed as if Kander hadn't been too kind to her friend, and it didn't surprise Charlie.

Raine had darker brown skin from her biracial background and was about three inches shorter than Charlie. Her tight, curly hair hung past her shoulders, but she kept it swept back with some old sunglasses. Her holey jeans and worn-out shirt were common for the humans on the planet. Moments ago, she had walked with a soft limp, but Charlie knew Raine's attitude would make up for any weakness. Strapped to her injured leg was an old laser gun that seemed to be reserved for her rowdier customers.

"What brings you back to Kander?"

"Business," Charlie replied.

Raine was about to ask more until she was cut off.

A passing Alpha yelled, "Fucking Betas."

Raine leaned to the right and shook a fist toward the passerby. "Come say that to my face!"

Charlie pivoted and narrowed her eyes at the Alpha's back. She noticed others in the market looked on for a moment. But it was her personal guard's smug look that irritated her the most. She turned back to Raine, switching back to English for privacy. "Betas?"

Raine placed her hands on her hips and sighed. "*It's some bullshit Kalmar slur for humans.*" She then glanced at her portable workbench that was littered with repairs. "*Maybe we can catch up later?*"

Charlie stiffened at the idea of reminiscing about the old days on Kander. It was easier to give false promise than refuse her sister. "*Sure.*" She considered the future and offered, "*Maybe after I get my job done.*" She took a step backward, closer to the crowd. "*Good to see you,* Raine," she called before vanishing among the people. Each bit of distance from her old friend helped ease the strain in her neck. However, her distraught nature caused her to crash into a rushing Alpha.

The Alpha dropped a clay bottle onto the cobblestones between his feet. The liquid splashed across the stones. The commotion had caught several passersby's attention.

Charlie backstepped and held up her hands. "*Perka gi,*" she apologized. "I didn't mean to—"

"You fucking Beta," the Alpha snarled.

Charlie lowered her hands, and her features twisted with anger after being called the slur again. She was accustomed to being called many things in many languages, but the Alpha's venomous tone made the slur feel like a weapon to Charlie. "Listen, it was an accident." She cursed at the empty holster at her side and no knife sheathed at her back.

The Alpha bared his teeth and edged closer to her. "All you Betas are an accident." He sniffed her scent, face twisting into disgust. "A disease on our planet."

Charlie frowned when all the other Kalmar backed away from the impending fight. She glanced over her shoulder at her guard, who stood indifferent about the situation. She cursed him for failing to perform his duty. With a bitter look, she refocused on the irate Alpha who loomed over her by a couple of feet. "But you don't seem to mind our tech." She indicated his wristband and then said, "Or our science."

The Alpha's lips curled up, and a low threatening sound rumbled in his chest as he took a step closer, hands at the ready. "All you fucking *females* believe you're Alphas when you're only Omegas with a mouth."

Rather than be baited, Charlie rolled her eyes at the Alpha and remarked, "At least we know how to use our mouths where it counts." Long ago she had learned what triggered Alphas, and now she was expecting him to be goaded into a fight. However, she was at a loss when the Alpha backed off and even shrank away from her. Then a raw power flowed over her and made her skin prickle with a warning. She was familiar with the sensation and knew who was behind her. A heavy sigh broke from her chest.

"Kal." The Alpha spoke with a tremble and bowed.

Kal stood behind Charlie and closed the space between them. "What is the problem?"

The Alpha explained the situation and became annoyed again when he looked at Charlie in front of Kal. After a moment, Kal turned toward Charlie's guard and commanded him to compensate the Alpha for his trouble. After the coin was handed over, she dismissed the Alpha to continue his personal business. Once he was gone, the onlookers started scattering and whispering among themselves.

Charlie glared at the departing Alpha. "I could have handled him."

"*Ja*, at my political expense," Kal stated.

Charlie hid a grin because Kal didn't argue with Charlie's abilities to battle the Alpha. She wanted to tease further, but Kal zeroed in on the guard.

"You were instructed to protect our guest."

The guard flexed his grip on the spear in his right hand but otherwise stared at his supreme leader. There was no denying his disobedience, and he seemed to accept his pending fate. Rather than a public punishment, Kal ordered him to return to the barracks. Later the guard would suffer a worse embarrassment among his squad.

Kal expelled a huff after the guard left and faced Charlie. "Where were you going?"

Charlie eyed Kal, then shrugged. "I was exploring the city. I've never seen Tarrak." She noticed a brief, puzzled look from Kal. "I've heard a lot about it."

Kal hummed low, then asked, "Perhaps you would enjoy seeing the Koblenz?"

Charlie perked up at the idea of seeing the river that flowed beside the famous capital, but she frowned and said, "I'm sure you have better things to do than play tour guide to a Beta." A displeased growl made her jump, and she tried easing her racing heart.

"The river is this way." Kal turned on her boots' heels and stomped off with raised shoulders.

After a grumble, Charlie followed alongside Kal. For several long minutes, she struggled with something to say, then hooked a strand of hair behind her left ear. The walk continued in silence, and it made Charlie tenser. Around them, the startled crowds hastened to part for their ruler.

"So I noticed a few human vendors in the market." Charlie counted at least twenty stands with human owners. It wasn't a lot compared to the few hundred stands, but not long ago, Earthlings weren't allowed in the city.

"*Ja*." Kal glanced at Charlie before looking ahead again. "I opened the market five years ago."

"Humans weren't allowed into the city before I left Kander."

"Much has changed since you left," Kal stated.

Charlie thought she heard a hint of pride in Kal's tone, and it made her smile a little. *What a typical Alpha*, she thought, then hesitated because Kal was indeed an Alpha but also rather different from the few she had met in the past. The distant look on her face faded away as the river came into view in front of them.

The Koblenz was a grand river with bluish-brown water that stretched on for long distances as it twisted its way through the capital's province until it poured into a bay that reached the sole ocean of the planet. Farther up, the river was narrow, but it widened as it approached the capital. It appeared to be half an old Earth mile wide at Tarrak's shores. On both sides of the shore were ports that allowed the transport of both goods and people through the provinces.

Kal brought Charlie to a relaxing spot along a cobblestone walkway. She approached a metal railing and placed her hands on it as she gazed upon the beautiful river. Beside her, Charlie smiled at the river and the city's ports around them.

"Amazing," Charlie whispered. She had heard stories about the wooden sailing ships in the ports. They reminded her of the ancient-style ships from the Greeks and Vikings of old Earth. They were wooden rather than made of some composite plastic material like fiberglass. However, these ships had mechanical engines that were solar powered when the winds were being less kind. Then there was the Koblenz itself, which was said to assist with powering the city. But Charlie was unsure how energy was harnessed from the river.

Kal hummed with pride for her planet's fleet, which had aided both the military and commerce over the generations. The Kalmar weren't considered the best seafaring race, but they managed to learn and took advantage of the waterways throughout their planet. The great dividing ocean was the only place where the Kalmar were less confident.

"I never took Kalmar for seamen," Charlie mentioned.

"We do prefer to keep our feet on the ground."

Charlie chuckled and thought of Starr, who hated flying, space, and water due to her hybrid nature. "Rarely the explorers."

Kal tilted her head, then said, "We do not have the human spirit of adventure."

Charlie shrugged and argued, "Not all humans are adventurous types." Then a grin played along her lips. "But certainly resilient."

Kal huffed, seeming to agree.

"Like a disease," Charlie whispered. "Like that Alpha said."

Grumbling low, Kal placed a hand on the railing and said, "It will take time for all my people to accept your people."

Charlie held up her hands, shook her head, and slapped her palms against the rail. "Not my people." She laughed without humor and explained, "I don't have any people. I'm just stuck as a human in this lifetime."

Kal fixed a curious stare on Charlie, who was still on the run from her heritage even as an adult. "Why did you leave Kander?"

"If you found a way to escape the war and bloodshed, wouldn't you take it?" Charlie lifted an eyebrow but didn't wait for an answer. "Never mind. You're a Kalmar and an Alpha." She looked over at the river and muttered, "You wouldn't get it."

Kal remained silent, but her features were thoughtful before she pushed Charlie further. "Did you not leave family behind?"

"*Joh*," Charlie denied and shook her head. "I have none." She shifted closer to the rail and leaned against it. Childhood memories from her past surfaced and forced her to relive the dark, oily confines of her life on the starship as it moved across the galaxy. "I grew up on the *Liberator*. Grew up around the engine intercooler system." She shook her head and said, "The cooling waste and recycling was awful. Today I can still smell the harsh chemicals of the cooling waste when I transported it for recycling."

"But then you grew up here on Kander," Kal reminded.

Charlie grunted and tried holding back memories from her years on Kander. Even if the planet was beautiful, her past was painted with blood and anger from both sides of the war. It was a wonder that she returned to Kander to take a job. Not wanting to think anymore on it, she turned to Kal. "How did you manage to stop the civil war? The last High Commander died from it."

"The last High Commander's usefulness had ended," Kal replied in an even tone. "The Spirit of Kalatas moved on to me because I strive for peace. I believe it is possible for Kalmar and Earthlings to live together."

"The last Kal didn't?"

"*Joh*, the last Kal's hatred spawned the war." Kal had a slight frown.

"You still didn't say how you managed to end the war."

With a heavy sigh, Kal explained, "I rooted out those who stood against a cease-fire."

After rubbing her brow, Charlie grumbled and said, "That sounds like a lot of bloodshed." The silence was confirmation enough. However, it was admirable that Kal was willing to find peace with the humans, and it meant their god accepted humans. In the beginning, many Kalmar wanted to purge the humans from Kander. It took great strength to rise above such hatred and bring any peace, even fragile peace.

A comfortable silence stretched on between them. Normally Kal stayed rigid in her posture, but she leaned against the railing. For a few more minutes, they enjoyed the quiet moment and were grateful to be out of the Great Tower.

"Can I ask you something personal?"

Kal straightened and inclined her head, giving permission.

"What's your name?" Charlie had leaned in closer to Kal, hoping to find out the secret. Perhaps it was taboo to ask, but she didn't give a damn. It wasn't like she was a citizen of the planet or under Kal's rule.

"It is Kal."

Charlie rolled her eyes and pushed off the rail after the failed attempt. Of course the High Commander of Kander would protect her real name. Kal had a role to play as a mortal god. Revealing her real name would shatter that mask.

"My name became Kal upon my ascension."

Charlie bit her bottom lip, then shook her head and tried one last time. "And your name before becoming Kal?" Again, she leaned in and waited for the secret.

"Upon my ascension, my old name left me." Kal appeared indifferent to the conversation and informed, "But it will return to me when Kalatas's spirit leaves me."

Eyeing Kal, Charlie wondered if it was part of a ploy or if Kal had forgotten her real name. Long ago she had learned that Kal was a god walking in mortal flesh among the Kalmar. Most of it was bullshit, in her humble opinion. But yet, those green eyes were a legend all their own. Every Kalmar had brown or black eyes but not Kal.

"Well…" Charlie continued staring deep into Kal's eyes, measuring for any truths but finding nothing. "I think you're a lot more than just a god." Not waiting for a response, she walked away from the rail and started in the direction of the Great Tower. After a moment, she found Kal accompanying her again.

"What language were you speaking to your crew? It is familiar."

"Jero?" Charlie shrugged and explained, "It's an old language from the Jerothian race. It's become the main, universal language in the galaxy." As they continued through the city, they remained in companionable silence until Kal was forced closer due to the busyness of the street, and they were at least another five minutes from the Great Tower.

"Does your crew know you lived on Kander?"

Charlie shrugged and sidestepped an overbearing Alpha who came near her. She received a light shove into Kal. For a tick, she swore Kal had snarled at the Alpha or perhaps at her. "Everyone knows Earthlings come from either Kander or Serrato. We don't talk much about our pasts. It's in the past for a reason." Starr was familiar with Charlie's past, but that wasn't Kal's business.

"The past tends to repeat if you ignore it," Kal stated.

Charlie gave a low laugh and shook her head. "Such a philosophical Alpha." Her path was cut off by Kal's much larger figure, and fear jolted every nerve in her body. Fiery green eyes made her heart pound in worry.

"Are you mocking my intelligence and my kind?" Kal's lips curled into a snarl.

Charlie swallowed at Kal's overbearing Alpha that she'd challenged with her smart comment. "*Joh*," she denied. "I just…" She let her explanation go after she realized her mistake in further challenging an Alpha—an

Alpha god. She bowed her head to pacify Kal and said, "*Perka gi.*"

After the apology, Kal expelled the air from her puffed-up chest and nodded in acceptance, then continued the walk to the Great Tower.

Once inside the building, they went to Charlie's room but parted ways after Charlie offered Kal a thank-you. A chill skated down Charlie's spine once she entered the bedroom, back slumped against the sealed door. Feeling the burn between her legs, she hated admitting her natural reaction to Kal. Charlie's head thudded against the door as she muttered, "Damn Alphas."

Chapter 4

"Y*ou grabbed everything we need?*" Charlie asked in Jero. She, Starr, and Raakor were gathered in Starr's room. Charlie had switched on her techbit's sound barrier for added protection. She placed the device on the table so it was centralized between them all.

Raakor nodded and tapped the techbit in his left hand, then pointed at the packs. "*Everything on the list minus the weapons they took.*" He returned his focus to his work on the device.

Starr grunted from her spot on the sofa. She was slumped against it, legs stretched out. Her mood was improved compared to yesterday.

Charlie gave a low huff of annoyance. It figured the damn Kalmar confiscated the extra weapons that Raakor had brought down from the *Pacifica*. "*Fuckin' bullshit.*" She continued grumbling while she went through the items.

"*Have you heard anything new?*"

Charlie glanced at Starr. "*Yes, actually.*" She drew the zipper down and closed the pack, then sat on the sofa next to Starr. "*Kal already contacted the kidnappers.*" She sighed at Starr's glower and further explained, "*Her ploy is that she's paying part of the ransom and killing the kidnappers when they show up to collect.*"

Raakor sat down in a wooden chair beside the sofa. "*Then what?*" He set the techbit on his thigh and studied Charlie.

"*Then you hack the ship's security, and we go after the Omega.*"

Starr hunched forward, elbows on her knees, and rubbed her forehead. "*Do we know what security system is on it?*" All of them were aware that Raakor would have to hack the system if they were going to utilize the kidnappers' ship.

"*No idea,*" Charlie admitted and cut her eyes over to Raakor, who rubbed his chin.

"*I don't know if I can hack the ship's security without first knowing what it is.*" Raakor sighed and stared at his boss.

"*I know.*" Charlie patted her knees and declared, "*We'll do our best.*" She hoped her confidence could settle her crewmen. They were between a rock and a hard place because Kal had plotted a trap.

"*And if that's not enough?*" Starr's voice rumbled with displeasure.

Charlie blew out a breath, then looked between the pair. "*Then we go to plan B.*" She received two glowers, so she shrugged and stated, "*We get in the* Pacifica *and find this Omega.*"

Starr groused further, stood, and remarked, "*This is a half-cocked plan.*" She started around the sofa, pacing behind it.

Charlie smiled at the words and joked, "*Fitting word considering it's an Alpha who did this.*"

Starr rolled her eyes and retorted, "*I highly doubt she's only halfway cocked.*"

Charlie's eyebrows hiked up, and she stared at Starr's tense back. But the sudden burn between her legs made her shift on the sofa. She faltered and cleared her throat before saying, "*It'll be fine.*" They had handled worse situations in the past. For once they were having the kidnappers delivered to them.

Starr had paced twice already between the sofa and bed. She grumbled and chewed on her bottom lip but paused and looked at Charlie. Her pending question was cut short by a knock on the door. In three wide strides, she jerked it open and barked, "What?"

"Kal has requested your boss's presence," Gaveston declared and eyed Starr from head to toe. The faint curl of his lip indicated his continued dislike for Starr.

Charlie jumped to her feet and was beside Starr. "I got this." She flashed a smile at Starr, who huffed and flashed her teeth at Gaveston. Then after a slight nod from Starr, Charlie slipped by and took Gaveston's side. In front of the door to Charlie's room stood a new guard, who was an Omega. Several questions hung at the tip of her tongue, but she swallowed them all down before she spoke.

"This way," Gaveston ordered and marched down the hallway. He moved at a fast pace, forcing Charlie to hurry. The new guard followed them and was on high alert compared to the previous one. Her footfall was also much lighter, and she had a confident air.

Charlie did her best not to peer back at the new guard. Once in the elevator, she stared ahead rather than at the guard. But from the corner of her eye, she gathered a few details.

The guard gripped a solid metal spear, which was more for symbol and status than practicality. However, the Kalmar were known to fight with melee weapons. Like other Kalmar soldiers, the guard carried a laser rifle across her back, and a long dagger was hooked to her left side. Her lengthy black shirt hugged every curve along her back and arms. Her patched-up pants were loose yet showed her more feminine curves. The one tiny bit of color in the guard's attire was the gray streak in her dark hair. Sensing Charlie's heavy stare, she turned her head sidelong and revealed a toothy smile.

The elevator hitched, then the guard drew open the gate. A little less distracted, Charlie gazed about her surroundings and realized they must have traveled up the Great Tower. In front of them were wooden double doors with heavy brass rings. It reminded her of the entrance to the throne room, but the windows to the left and right weren't there last time. They were on a different floor. Two guards dipped their heads at the newcomers, and one grabbed onto a ring. The left door creaked low and swung open halfway.

This time, Charlie eyed Gaveston to ensure he didn't attempt to shove her again. She stepped around him and entered the room alone, the door shutting behind her. Inside the room, there was a long lounge sofa with no back and a wooden coffee table in front of it. Two worn leather sofas were flanked on either side of the lounger. In front of the furniture was a fireplace with an animal fur spread across the stone floor.

A soft sound from the other room came through the doorway and drew Charlie to the opening. As she approached, she called in Kalmarese, "*Turen*?" She paused at the doorframe, hand resting on the side, then repeated her greeting. "*Turen*?" With a slow scan, she started taking in the bedroom until a sliding door on the left opened. Charlie's heart jumped into her throat before it dropped and thundered against her chest.

Coming out of the bathroom, Kal halted and went still upon seeing Charlie in the doorway. From her head to her feet, she was devoid of any shred of clothing. There was nothing within reach to cover herself. Somehow she managed to keep a neutral expression compared to Charlie.

"Oh my gods!" Charlie gasped after snapping her jaw shut, only to have it fall open again. She gaped at the nude Alpha with a keen interest. Before her was a gorgeous sight that she devoured in detail. Kal's breasts were full, then her stomach muscles were finely sculpted and made Charlie's palms itch with desire. But lower still, Charlie's full attention was claimed by the most unexpected surprise of all. She choked at the sight of the semihard cock between two powerful thighs.

"I..."

Kal groused and demanded, "Do all humans refuse to knock?"

Charlie was tongue-tied but gained a measure of self-control, lifting her eyes back up to Kal's displeased features. She became more aware of herself and spun around while apologizing, "*Perka gi.*" She touched her forehead. "I'll wait in the sitting room." She retreated from the bedroom, but the mental image of Kal was seared in her memory.

Sinking into the sofa, Charlie bent forward with her elbows on her knees and hands over her face. Heat continued pulsing through her cheeks and made it even harder to calm down. "Oh gods. I'm never going to unsee that," she muttered, now having her answer about what kind of equipment the High Commander had between her legs. Well, as much as an answer as possible since it was from a distance. She tried to wipe away the incident, but it was useless. The warmth in her face started spreading through her, then a dull ache pulsed between her legs.

Soft footfall forced her to focus on the present. Kal sat next to her, which triggered the heat in her face to radiate more. Charlie considered scooting away but stayed, not wanting to be rude or irritate Kal any further. Kal had dressed in loose black pants and a deep-red tank top, with nothing on her feet. Her untamed hair was still damp.

"You uh…" Charlie fidgeted with the buckle of her utility belt. "You asked to see me." Even to her own ears, she sounded idiotic and groaned at herself.

Kal tilted her head, then mentioned, "The kidnappers responded to my message."

The news made Charlie perk up and helped her focus. The wonderful throb between her legs dulled to a soft burn.

"They wish to move forward with the first stage of the ransom."

"That's good." Charlie revealed a devious smile. If the kidnappers fell for the trap, there was hope that it could work. Raakor was worried about hacking the ship's flight system, but it was an older ship. She doubted anyone had upgraded the flight system to a newer one. It would be stupid to throw away good stills into such an ancient boat. If that was the case, then the flight system would be easier to crack. "When will they be here?"

"In a day's time."

Charlie chewed on her bottom lip and stared down at her hands on her knees. She hoped that was enough time for Starr's flare-up to end or at least relent to a degree. After a deep breath, she regarded Kal and asked, "Where do we meet them?"

"The location has not been decided yet."

"It'll probably be a remote spot," Charlie whispered. "And only so many soldiers."

"I doubt it will be too remote. But perhaps a more open location." Kal canted her head and added, "Soldiers are forbidden, and I am to deliver the darakar alone to them."

Charlie attempted to focus on Kal's face, but her attention crept to Kal's exposed biceps. They were large and well formed, requiring many hours of hard work to build up. She wanted to squeeze one and confirm their solidness. Fighting back a blush, she cleared her throat and argued, "That's a little dangerous."

After a low noise of agreement, Kal stated, "I must think on this."

"Think quickly," Charlie suggested. "There's not much time." She pursed her lips and weighed different options. "Maybe they will negotiate on the soldiers, especially if they want the first load of fuel."

Kal was quiet, then nodded in agreement at the idea.

"Is the darakar even ready?" Charlie was aware that mining and refining the fuel was no simple task. But the Kalmar were known for stockpiling the fuel. No one had an idea how much, but Charlie wouldn't be surprised if it was enough to power a fleet or two.

"*Ja*." Kal had a brief frown that caught Charlie off guard. She left Charlie on the couch and neared the unlit fireplace. "We will discuss this further tomorrow."

Charlie withheld from rolling her eyes at Kal's need to plot and scheme, alone. After a sigh, she stood and neared Kal. The earlier memory of finding Kal nude in the bedroom crept to the forefront of her mind. She fought against blushing more, but it was a losing battle.

Even now, the amount of bare skin from Kal was teasing Charlie. By nature, most Alphas were muscular and well-built, especially those in the military. Kal was no exception and was a prime example of power and strength. If Kal wanted to, she could pick up Charlie without a single strain. The alluring thought tempted Charlie to whimper. She held it back, until Kal leaned into her space.

Kal's face hovered alongside Charlie's cheek. She breathed in, deep and long, scenting Charlie. Charlie's heart lurched into light speed. She told herself to withdraw, but she was frozen under Kal's scrutiny. Her scent carried tidbits of information that Kal's sensitive nose would analyze. Charlie was certain her arousal was the most prominent note. A terrible tremble passed through her when low rumbles echoed through the room.

For several more ticks, Kal loomed close but didn't touch Charlie. She inched her nose lower, closer to Charlie's neck. After an agonizing minute, Kal lifted her head until her lips were a hair's breadth from a flushed ear. "At twenty-one hundred, the guards at my doors will go off duty," Kal whispered.

Charlie fisted her shaking hands, keeping herself from grabbing onto Kal for support. Her next breath hitched in her throat when Kal's rumbly voice thundered in her ear again.

"Your guard will bring you here, if you wish."

Staring at Kal, Charlie tried to grasp the meaning behind the unspoken offer. She was a human and Kal a Kalmar. Why would such a powerful Alpha want to bed someone like Charlie? If word spread about the High Commander fucking a human, then Kander might implode. With a sliver of clarity, she murmured, "It's too dangerous for me *and* you."

Like a ghost, Kal brushed the tip of her nose along the curve of Charlie's reddened ear. A delightful chill zipped down Charlie's spine. "Nothing will leave this room," she swore to Charlie. A low thrum shook in her chest before she whispered, "I swear it." She withdrew.

Charlie's eyes fluttered a few times as Kal receded, with the spicy Alpha scent retreating from under her nose. If it was kept quiet, then it was harmless fun. Besides, it was one night that would be forgotten once Charlie flew off at the end of her completed mission. Once upon a time, Charlie would have sex with a client, if they piqued her interest. And well, Kal had more than caught Charlie's eye. After a deep breath, she forced her legs to work and take her to the front doors.

Kal remained quiet and pulled open a door, holding it until Charlie was gone. Unsure how to answer, Charlie departed from the quarters but paused in the corridor. She gazed over her shoulder and shivered when she received a wolfish smile from Kal. She struggled against the burning attraction swelling in her. Needing space, she hurried off and followed her guard into the waiting elevator. Silence stayed between them during the entire trip back to her room. She ignored her guard's curious sniff. Once alone in her room, she collapsed into a chair beside the cold, unlit fireplace.

Charlie recalled her memory of the High Commander, naked and on display. She indulged in a dirty little fantasy of being braver and touching Kal while she stood there. In her daydream, Charlie traced every muscle's curve and felt the weight of Kal's breasts in her palms. Then Charlie gave her full attention to the lengthy shaft between Kal's legs. She might have not seen it in great detail, but Charlie pictured its erect stance and dripping head.

Slouched against the chair, Charlie covered her face and fought to end the fantasy. She was too aroused. Her pussy was soaked while her clitoris throbbed with hot demand. How was she supposed to be around her crewmen after dinner if she was wired? Plus Starr might notice Charlie's state, especially in her hypersensitive mode.

Yet, Charlie considered Kal's unique biology. Kal was a unique blend of both sexes, at least human sexes. Kalmar were not humans and didn't use terms such as "man" or "woman" in their language. They were split up between Alpha and Omega breeds. However, Kal was a bit of both. Charlie had learned a lot about the Kalmar during her childhood, but she had missed the stories about Kal's special breed.

Then there was Kal's delicate offer on the table. Over the years, Charlie had slept with women, men, intersex, and other types of sexes among various species. After feeling brow ridges, extra hands, scales, leathery skin, and tails, these days very little rattled her. A lover was only as good as their skill with their own equipment during sex. Someone such as Kal, a being of power, had to be skilled with her equipment, or so Charlie hoped.

However, one night with Kal could prove to be fatal for them both. The war between Kalmar and Earthlings ceased years ago, but it did nothing to end the continued animosity toward humans on Kander. The refugee Earthlings on Kander were still segregated from the Kalmar, and tolerances for human and Kalmar interactions had apparently improved by only minuscule amounts, if the latest slur of "Beta" was any indication. It was considered a sin and a breach in Kalmar honor for a Kalmar and a human to share a bed. With such political and personal ramifications, Charlie questioned why Kal was willing to risk everything. In truth, it was pure suicide for Kal.

And yet, an offer for sex with Kal was rather enticing. Charlie was willing to cross the line even if it was dangerous. Ever since the first meeting, Charlie felt drawn to Kal, like a taut rope that was reeling her in closer with every encounter. She had met Alphas in the past and learned they were all the same, aggressive, brooding assholes who could only be tamed by an Omega, not by a human.

Kal appeared cold and hard, a god for her people and the strongest Alpha. At least until Charlie paid closer attention. Behind the frozen exterior was a spark of life, of humility, an individual. There was more to Kal than an Alpha god who walked with the mortals. It was also clear that Kal retained some mortal desires.

Charlie rose from the chair and went to the sealed windows on the other side of the room. She nudged one open, and the cool air soothed her flushed features, easing her wandering mind. The suns hugged the horizon, indicating the arrival of dinner. When the meal was brought into her room, she ignored it and muttered a thank-you to the servant.

At twenty hundred, she stepped out of her room and traded a glance with the Omega guard, who raised an eyebrow at her. After a grumble, she knocked on Raakor's door and had him join her and Starr in one room. As a team, they circled around the small living space in Starr's room. Once a sound barrier was set up, Charlie started explaining the current news and worried her bottom lip when her crew stayed quiet at the end.

"*This isn't ideal,*" Charlie admitted in Jero after the too-long silence from her crew. "*I get it. But the ship looked older, and I think it'll have a more basic flight system.*"

Starr's low grunt was the first response.

Raakor stared at the tattoos on his skin, as if tracing them with his eyes. "*That is true.*" He lifted his gaze to Charlie and added, "*Unless they have updated it.*"

"*From the photos, that boat looks pretty rough.*"

Raakor nodded while Starr shook her head and asked, "*What if they don't show up in that ship?*"

Bobbing her head, Charlie thought about the possibility. "*They might not. But it was a transporter ship, which would be ideal for moving the darakar.*" She hoped her logic would ease her crewmen. "*We can handle this.*" They had a backup plan and would complete the mission. They didn't have a choice in the end.

"*The High Commander is a controlling asshole,*" Starr said and left the sofa, stomping over to the lit fireplace.

Charlie grunted and had little to no argument with Starr's keen observation. She remained on the couch but focused on Raakor. "*Starr and I will probably pose as soldiers so we can help Kal.*"

Raakor indicated his purple skin, which reminded them of his inability to blend in as a Kalmar.

After a grin, Charlie became serious and said, "*After you hack the kidnappers' ship, you'll take the shuttle back up to the* Pacifica."

Raakor nodded. "*Honestly, it's not a horrible plan.*"

"*But it hinges on you being able to crack the ship's flight system security,*" Starr said and turned toward the pair. "*And who knows what the fuck they use.*"

"*It could be any AI system like Ravage, Cybertronics, or the Gyr's system.*" There were many more on the list than what Raakor had named.

Charlie sighed at all the possibilities. Many of them Raakor knew well, but even he had limits. "*You may have to take the lead with the* Pacifica, *depending what the kidnappers' ship has for navigation.*"

Raakor lifted his black eyes to his leader and gave a low nod.

"*How's your flare-up?*"

Starr pulled her attention from the burning fireplace to Charlie and replied, "*On the downside.*" There were some miracles after all.

"*Good.*" Charlie stood up with the techbit in her right hand and noticed it was late. "*I'm going to get some rest.*" She removed the sound barrier and exchanged a goodnight with her team before leaving the room.

Disregarding the Omega guard, Charlie vanished into her room, paced the small room, and weighed the pros and cons about tonight. Did Kal feel any measure of anxiety about Charlie's pending decision? The fireplace responded with a soft crackle, then the open and close of a door told her Raakor had departed Starr's room. It was almost twenty-one hundred, but Charlie was indecisive about Kal's offer. Her common sense was at war with her attraction toward Kal. Even if someone learned about the one-night stand, it wouldn't be Charlie's problem since she had nothing to do with Kander. If Kal felt safe enough to make the offer, then Charlie was stupid for worrying about the consequences.

Besides, how many people had the chance to fuck the High Commander of Kander?

Chapter 5

"I wish to see Kal."

The Omega guard remained stationary other than the slight rise of her chest, until she gave the faintest of nods. She peeled herself off the stone wall and led the way to the lift that would take them up to Kal.

Charlie clenched and unclenched her hands with each tick. She caught herself from colliding into the guard, who turned to shut the elevator gate. She chose to ignore the guard's dark smirk. Whether the guard knew why Charlie was going to Kal at night was the least of her concerns. In truth, she was unsure whether she wanted to know that the guard had received orders to allow Charlie to visit Kal.

As the lift hitched at the second-to-top floor, Charlie blew out a low breath and followed the guard to the sealed doors. The two guards were indeed gone, and the soft light from the overhead torches was the welcoming sign. Her guard rapped on a door and stepped aside when the left door creaked open with Kal on the other side. She bowed her head to her ruler, then shifted and presented Charlie.

Perhaps it wasn't the first time that the guard had brought Kal a bedmate. Shaking off the idea, Charlie clenched her hands when Kal's intense eyes locked on her. Under the burning gaze, she felt bare and spread open, unsure how to handle the situation.

"Return to your post at our guest's room."

"*Ja*, Kal." After a final bow, the guard returned to the waiting elevator and left them alone.

Kal reversed and drew the door wider, inviting Charlie to enter her quarters.

Once Charlie passed the threshold, the heavy door closed behind her. All of Kal's attention remained on her, as if she was measuring and scheming the night's plan. Sparks of panic flared up in Charlie's chest, and her breaths grew heavier. Standing there, she worried she'd chosen poorly tonight. Kal had been reserved in their previous interactions, until now. The openness was subtle, but the change was noticeable. Kal gazed upon Charlie with wolfish hunger, as if she'd waited years for Charlie.

But then the spell was broken. Kal went to the bedroom and glanced back at Charlie. She still wore the same clothes from earlier. Her hair was dry, with one braid on either side to hold it back. Her bare feet were quiet against the stone flooring.

After a deep breath, Charlie followed into the candlelit room and needed a moment for her eyes to adjust to the warm glow. Unsure of what to do, she fidgeted with her utility belt and waited for Kal's move. She stiffened when Kal stepped into her personal space yet managed to keep a sliver of space between them. Kal bent over Charlie, scenting her again. A low, pleased purr vibrated deep in her chest.

Charlie reached for Kal's arms but dropped her hand and looked over at the large bed next to her. She groaned after picturing them naked and kissing. Her groan shifted to a grumble when she recalled that Kalmar weren't kissers and were uninterested in using their mouths. They were dominated by smells and bites—lots of biting. Kal's low grunt recalled her attention.

"Remove your clothes first," Kal ordered. "Our scents will cross otherwise."

Charlie swallowed first, then gave a nod. Other Kalmar would smell their crossed and aroused scents if they touched while wearing clothes. However, the confidence to strip down was absent for Charlie, who floundered when Kal pulled off her own tank top and revealed her toned abs.

Kal had backed off, putting space between them. She tossed the tank top onto a wing chair beside a bench, revealing her bare upper body. Every muscle down her arms and sculpted line across her stomach was highlighted with the glow from the candlelight. Her nipples were hard from the cooler air. For a moment, she hooked her thumb at the waistband of her pants, waiting for Charlie.

Charlie coached herself. She had multiple sexual partners in the past and was experienced. Her attempt to boost her confidence faltered at the thought of bedding an Alpha for the first time. People didn't bed Alphas; the Alpha bedded them. She remained disjointed, lost to Kal's presence and command. She reached for the hem of her black shirt, peeling it off before dropping it to the floor. She knelt to remove her boots.

Kal's eyes had lost their color, blown with passion. Her lips curled to reveal the sharpness of her prominent canines. Charlie had lovers who'd shown her sexual desire, but Kal was raw and primal. Were all Alphas so predatory or was it only Kal? Charlie fumbled with the buckle of her utility belt. Kal fisted her hand and grew rumbly. Spicy waves of pheromones poured from her and distracted Charlie.

Trying to move faster, Charlie stepped out of her pants and dropped them with a heavy thud. She stood before Kal in her bra and underwear, vulnerable in every way. Kal's jaw was clenched and her knuckles white. For an Alpha, she displayed more restraint than Charlie expected.

"Everything," Kal ordered in a growly tone.

After licking her lips, Charlie nodded and undid the bra before she touched the soft underwear. Hooking her fingers into them, she dragged them off, and the cool air brushed against the dampness between her legs. Her eyelashes fluttered when Kal gave a pleased noise. Sparks danced deeper in her gut.

Upon opening her eyes, she became aware of the visible bulge between Kal's legs. The loose black pants did nothing to hide Kal's hard attraction. Charlie bit her lip when Kal pushed the waistband down, creeping lower until the stiff cock was freed from its confines. Being so much closer gave Charlie a better view of finer details, like the fact Kal had no visible testicles. But she wasn't naive enough to think that she couldn't get pregnant by a female

Alpha. Years ago, she had started using an injectable contraceptive that protected her.

With the pants off, Kal added them to the tank top on the chair, then looked at Charlie's flushed features. With a single step, she closed the gap between her and Charlie, who grabbed onto thick, coiled biceps. Before she could speak, sharp teeth latched onto her neck and blazed a trail across her delicate flesh. "*Fuck*," Charlie whispered in English and dug her nails into tense muscle. Kal pressed closer, making her thick shaft even more apparent. Droplets of her slick smeared against Charlie's stomach.

"Get onto the bed." Kal pushed Charlie backward and grazed her teeth over a soft ear. Her breaths were hot and sent chills across Charlie's shoulders.

Charlie grunted when her ass bumped the firm bed. With a yank of her head, she freed herself from the nipping teeth. Everything was happening fast and control was slipping from her hands, if she ever had any. Her fiery gaze halted Kal, long enough for her to speak up. "If you think you're going to rut into me like a piece of meat, you're fucking wrong." She increased her grip on Kal's thick arms and did her best to ignore all the power of an Alpha god bearing down on her. But a warning growl took the strength out of her knees.

Kal flashed her teeth and forced Charlie onto the bed. Reclined on her back, Charlie scrambled away on her hands. But Kal followed like a wolf cornering its prey. Her snarl was thick and endless even when their faces were separated by a breath. She had crawled over Charlie's prone form.

Charlie attempted to push against Kal's broad shoulder. Wrangling for dominance, she showed her own display of teeth in silent rebellion. She dared Kal to push the limits further, but the longer she stared into those eyes, the more she lost her resolve. Her hints of fear were mixed with the thick arousal that continued to pool between her legs. Trembles started low in her belly, passing up to her arms and showing Kal her weakness.

Kal had her hands anchored to the bed on either side of Charlie. She continued holding Charlie's stare, daring her to fight more. Days ago Kal had been a calm, rational being, but not tonight. She seemed a bit unhinged, perhaps by Charlie's mere presence. Charlie sensed that rejecting Kal might undo a thin line of self-restraint in Kal. When the ticks passed without any more argument, Kal rocked back onto her knees, snared Charlie's sides, and turned her over.

Charlie was unprepared for the change, and panic exploded into terror at the thought of being dominated. There was no way in hell she could allow somebody, especially an Alpha, to take her from behind. She yelled and grappled with Kal despite her losing chances.

Rumbles and growls erupted from Kal as she fought with Charlie. Their hands slid, and her feet jammed into Kal's solid stomach, but the Alpha was like a vice that gripped down. Kal had Charlie on her belly and snared her thick arms around Charlie. She lifted Charlie's upper body until their bodies molded together.

A strained cry broke from Charlie, and she pushed against the thick coils of muscle across her chest and stomach that had her locked in place. For the first time, she was powerless in bed and afraid of what Kal may do to her. She was idiotic to think having sex with a Kalmar Alpha was sane, much less safe.

Kal released a low huff near Charlie's ear, then snarled, "I will not hurt you." Behind the roughness was a warmth that penetrated Charlie's irrational emotions.

Somehow the promise ended Charlie's fight. She took a deep breath, dropped her head against the broad shoulder behind her, and regained her better senses. The gentle rumbles at her back calmed her further and chased off the last of the panic in her bones. A different kind of tremble started throughout her body as she accepted that Kal might be careful with her.

In every sexual encounter, Charlie had been in command and had rules, never trusting anyone wholly. But this Alpha, a mortal god called Kal, was demanding she let go, and for once the noise in her head died off. She released another heavy breath, losing a weight on her shoulders and withdrawing her nails from the arms around her body.

As if sensing the shift, Kal lowered them to the bed, bodies never breaking apart. She pressed her right hand against the bed while her left arm remained hooked around Charlie's stomach. She remained curled over Charlie, breathing in her scent, never seeming to get enough.

Charlie moved her hair to one side and bit her lip when Kal nuzzled her ear. Such a small gesture eased her nerves even more, and she wondered if there was indeed a softer side to Alphas.

Kal nudged the reddened ear one last time before whispering, "I am going to fuck you and keep fucking you until you tell me to stop." Her teeth grazed across the tip of the ear while Charlie groaned in response.

"Just…" Charlie stumbled over her words, mouth dry as a desert. "Just go slow at first." Earlier she had seen the size of Kal's cock, which would require time to adjust to, if possible. The old gossip about the size of Alpha dicks was indeed true. She swallowed when Kal pulled her left arm free. Together, they shifted until Charlie was on her hands and knees with Kal behind her. She expected to be taken and filled without consideration, but instead, the thick length between her ass cheeks was pulled away. Instead, Kal nudged her cock between Charlie's legs, under her pussy.

Kal returned her arm around Charlie's stomach and nipped against warm skin along Charlie's shoulders. She rolled her hips, and a soft rumble passed from her into Charlie. Her cock pushed back and forth, the movements brushing Charlie's throbbing clit. With a gasp, Charlie curled her fingers into the bed's cover and struggled with her body's natural desire to rock her hips too.

"Relax," Kal ordered in a thick voice.

Nodding, Charlie gave in to her needs and moved her hips with Kal's own. Her sensitive clit rubbed against the hardened length, spreading slickness along her inner thighs. Each push back caused the cock's head to tap against her belly. Her own wetness smeared down the shaft, making it even easier to grind together. Their sweat mingled, and her whimpers mixed with demanding Alpha growls. Every pass across her clit built her up more and more.

Kal snared Charlie's hip and halted her. Her snarl deepened and passed through Charlie. She released Charlie, withdrew a little, and moved her hand between their bodies. Charlie hissed at the loss of contact but trembled from what was to follow. The ache in her pussy made her impatient. Kal tapped her arm against Charlie's ass a few times, stroking her cock to make sure it was hard enough for Charlie.

Charlie clenched her bottom lip, withholding her verbal demand that Kal fill her. She wiggled her ass in an attempt to hurry Kal. She had wanted sex in the past, but tonight she was consumed by a new level of need, one almost foreign to her. When the tip of Kal's shaft kissed her entrance, she groaned in both excitement and gratefulness.

As promised, Kal went slow and gentle as she pressed her right hand flat against Charlie's stomach, bracing her. At a painstaking speed, she eased her hips forward and nudged the tip of her cock past the entrance.

Charlie's low gasp made her growl, perhaps in self-restraint more than anything. She continued easing farther into Charlie's tight depths.

Each push forward caused Charlie to whimper and claw more into the bed cover. The earlier emptiness was replaced by the slow but exquisite fullness. Every time Kal reached farther into her, she felt another emotion rise in her chest. A slight burn started around her entrance, and the next push made her latch onto Kal's wrist, a silent plea for her to pause.

Seeming to understand, Kal stopped but leaned down again until her front pressed into Charlie's sticky back. She used her left hand to balance her larger weight. Never moving forward or backward, she remained still inside Charlie, showing both restraint and consideration.

"How far are you in?" Charlie asked, short of breath.

"It does not matter." Kal bit the skin along Charlie's neck and down her shoulder. The attention distracted Charlie from the demanding stretch inside her. Too curious, Charlie reached back and grazed the portion of Kal's length that remained out of her. She huffed at the possible incompatibility issues between them. Sensing her displeasure, Kal nudged her cock and broke Charlie's negative thoughts until a brief thought dashed through her mind.

"Can you knot me?" Charlie blurted out. Alphas had to be in a rut to form a knot, but Charlie had no idea if it was the same for Kal's unusual breed. Kal's amused rumble transferred through Charlie's entire frame, surprising her. The sound sent an excited chill down her spine.

"I am not in a rut."

A blush colored Charlie's cheeks. She retorted, "You *are* a little big." A warm huff brushed across her ear followed by a thick chuckle, but all amusement vanished when Kal drew her cock back out. Heat started to rebuild low in Charlie's gut.

Every precious measure of thickness slid from Charlie's tightened walls, closer to her entrance. Each movement forced her fingers to twist deeper into the sheets. After she drew in a sharp breath, Kal stopped and kept her cockhead at Charlie's G-spot. Kal's ability to go slow was both perfect and maddening for Charlie.

The wait for Kal to push in again nearly drove Charlie to beg and plead. To her relief, Kal urged her hips forward and reclaimed Charlie's silky tightness. Charlie dropped her head and panted against the building need.

Once Kal reached Charlie's limit, they groaned together. But Charlie wanted to take more and tried to rock backward and grind on the hard length. A sudden sting flared along her neck when Kal's canine teeth clamped on her skin. Charlie stiffened and whimpered after receiving a warning. She grabbed onto Kal's nearby wrist. Kal was reinforcing her control over their current arrangement, making Charlie submit.

"You are still too tight for any more."

Charlie swallowed and nodded in agreement but insisted, "But we can go faster." A gentle nip against her shoulder made her shiver and left prickles on her skin.

Kal lifted her head and adjusted her position, preparing to fulfill Charlie's wish. With more speed, she withdrew her cock and drove right back into the tight walls. This time there was no testing or conversation. Kal snapped her hips back, dragging her hardened length through the wet heat. Charlie's whine seemed to encourage Kal further, the speed increasing with each thrust.

Sweat beaded down Charlie's brow and across her back. With her teeth clamped over her lip, she muffled the soft cries and clawed harder against the bed. Lust burned thick in her belly, and each new push became a little deeper, building her up more.

"You do not..." Kal faltered thrusts but ordered, "Do not be silent." She clawed one of Charlie's ass cheeks and promised, "You are safe here."

Charlie was flooded with relief, unsure if she could have withheld her cries of pleasure much longer. Kal's pumping hips and girthy length were too glorious. She released her lip and let out the first cry.

"Much better," Kal praised Charlie, who moaned from the encouragement. Kal then shifted her knees against the bed, better bracing herself. She increased the pace and drove into Charlie, again and again. Her grunts turned into light howls with each stroke, but she never buried her full length into Charlie.

Still, the lust and pleasure shot through them and made Charlie cry out, wanting the satisfaction. Needing the last measure, she rocked back against Kal and forced the thrusts deeper, sending heated bolts up into her chest. Charlie let out a delightful whimper with every pump until Kal's final one split her open. She screamed, matching her Alpha lover's howl. Weakened, Charlie started to crumble toward the bed, but Kal caught her. Together, they eased down to the furs and blankets without breaking their contact.

Kal pressed against Charlie's back, but Kal's full weight wasn't baring down on her. Like Charlie, she heaved and trembled after the mutual climax. She took deeper breaths and pressed her nose into Charlie's hair. After a minute, she started to purr and rubbed her hips against Charlie's ass. Her cock massaged against Charlie's walls before she withdrew. Charlie was almost certain that Kal was still hard.

Charlie regained her senses even as the orgasm continued tingling low in her belly. After a deep breath, she twisted her head toward Kal, who held her gaze. Under the soft light, Kal's eyes appeared cool, but there was something else deeper in them. Perhaps it was the echoes of a mortal Alpha who continued to live on under her godly armor. Or could Kal be recalling her old name and life, a person that Charlie realized she wished to know? Without thought, she reached and grazed a flushed cheek with her fingertips, as if she could free the mortal buried under the god.

Kal captured the smaller hand into hers, leaned closer, and asked, "Will you leave now?"

Kal's thick voice curled around Charlie's heart, slurring the next beat. She weighed the true depth of Kal's question and released a breath as her common sense lost the battle. A string coiled around Charlie's emotions, and she murmured, "*Joh.*"

Kal revealed a devilish smile and let out a pleased noise, which caused the slickness to return between Charlie's legs. She snaked her arm around Charlie's waist and lifted them both until they were seated upright. Kal's lap was damp from both sweat and slick.

Charlie released a shaken breath before leaning back into Kal's sturdy frame. Kal was propped up by her outstretched arms, leaving her hands indisposed. A gentle nudge to Charlie's flushed cheek encouraged her to take some control, which made her stomach twist. She dug her nails into Kal's muscular thighs, unsure of herself.

Kal lifted, freeing her left hand and brushing pale strands off Charlie's scarred shoulder. She nuzzled Charlie but trailed her lips back, breathing into the shell of Charlie's ear. When Charlie shuddered against her, she growled and bit the earlobe under her tongue. Charlie clawed into muscles, but Kal snared one of Charlie's wrists and their hands to Charlie's lap. Their fingertips grazed the glistening blond between her legs, teasing her.

"Kalmar are never slick here," Kal whispered into Charlie's ear. "Only in here." She guided two of their fingers to the opening in her pussy.

Charlie panted and leaned against Kal, eyes heavy. She struggled to register the tidbit of education about Omegas. "Is there anything else different?"

Kal canted her head, then trailed their fingers between Charlie's slick pussy lips until they brushed her hard clitoris. The delicate touch sent a ripple of pleasure through her.

"This bump. Omegas have nothing here."

Charlie gasped and tried keeping her composure, even if her body betrayed her. "Humans call it a *clitoris* or a *clit*," she explained, using English terms. She clenched her lip between her teeth when Kal rubbed her thumb across her clit, testing both it and her. Her groan was loud, and she wanted Kal to keep touching her.

Kal bowed her head and pressed her lips against Charlie's neck, tasting her. Her tongue mimicked the same pattern her thumb drew against Charlie's clit. "So sensitive," she said before applying more pressure to Charlie's swollen bud.

"*Vuk*," Charlie cursed after Kal's thumb rolled across her clit again. She withdrew her own hand and pressed it against the bed for support. The next caress encouraged her to spread her legs farther, past Kal's hips. Her unspoken invite seemed to evoke a pleased sound from Kal. She dropped her head against a large shoulder and allowed her Alpha lover to play with her.

Kal pulled her thumb up and down against the silky pearl, learning Charlie's reaction. A few times her finger slipped from all the wetness. "You are very slick." Her words held a thread of awe and praise, causing Charlie to shiver.

With her right arm adjusted for better support, Charlie returned her other hand to her lap and reached for her own labia. With two fingers, she spread herself open in offer and gave her lover better access. She needed Kal to keep learning her clit, and each stroke made her insides clench harder.

Kal purred into Charlie's ear and switched to her index finger, rubbing the wet and swollen bud. Her motions were less uncertain and held more demand. Even if Kal was new to Charlie's human anatomy, she learned what pushed Charlie closer to the edge.

Charlie's urgency for an orgasm took command. She rolled her hips and worked her clitoris against Kal's touch. She clenched her teeth and ordered, "Push down more."

Kal growled in return and applied firm pressure to Charlie's clit, shooting passion up Charlie's spine. She clamped an arm around Charlie's midsection and held her in place.

"Faster," Charlie demanded and strained against Kal's hold. She clawed the fur and peered down at Kal's hand between her legs, working to please her. Her attention trailed to Kal's cock, which peeked out between Charlie's spread out thighs. The glistening head was enflamed and swollen while a droplet beaded at the tip. "*Vuk*," she hissed a moment before the orgasm undid her. Charlie screamed then yelped when Kal's teeth clamped onto the side of her neck, in a pleasurable hold.

For a while, Charlie rested against her lover, savoring the bliss humming under the skin and the hold of Kal's teeth on her flesh. After a minute, a mildly rough tongue soothed the bite and made Charlie moan. Never had she allowed anyone to bite her in such a manner, and she was thankful that an Alpha had been her first. A Kalmar understood exactly where to bite, how hard, and for how long to not only please their lover but also to speak to them.

After a deep breath, Charlie lifted her head and studied Kal's hand resting on her pale stomach. Further past their laps was the hard cock that had tipped her over the edge earlier. Another greedy twinge started low in her gut, and her entrance throbbed with want. She inhaled and whispered, "I need you in me again."

For the second time, Kal gave a chuckle, and it was heavy enough to pass into Charlie's body. Responding to Charlie's demand, she removed her touch from Charlie's stomach, placed it behind herself again, and nudged her hips against Charlie's ass. It was a silent challenge for Charlie to take it if she wanted it.

Lust heated Charlie's belly. Her glistening skin flushed with desire, and she was the slickest she had ever been in her life. She was enveloped in Kal's heady scent that excited and comforted her. Unable to resist, Charlie wrapped her hand around the thick shaft. Kal's throaty moan encouraged her further. She trembled and massaged the shaft, listening to Kal's responses. For a moment, the temptation to taste the droplets of slick overwhelmed her. She hesitated and grappled with the strange yearning to give oral sex.

Catching the cockhead in her palm, Charlie held it, then scooted her hips forward until her pussy grazed the base. Kal groaned in Charlie's ear, but allowed Charlie to have her fun. With a grin, she rocked her hips and rubbed her pussy along the hard length. The few ropey veins grazed across her clitoris, drawing out a long moan from her.

Every drop of arousal that transferred onto Kal's cock would make it easier for Charlie to ride her. After a few more strokes, she moved her hand to the base, shifted forward, and lifted herself up and over the tip. Kal held on to Charlie's sides, guiding her. She should have gone slower, adjusting to the stretch, but Charlie was too greedy and took all she could in a single stroke.

Kal trembled and dug her fingers into Charlie's skin. But she refrained from taking charge. Her self-control as an Alpha was attractive and secretly heartwarming.

Using her arms and legs, Charlie started the mindless fucking. She tilted her head back and moaned louder with each downstroke. The incredible fullness stole her breath. Her body radiated with searing pleasure while Kal grunted in her ear. The chase for an orgasm put a strain on her arms. Charlie slowed and whined until Kal seemed to read her mind.

With a few adjustments, Kal lifted Charlie from her lap, hooked her left arm under Charlie's knees, and clutched her right hand under Charlie's ass. She had

Charlie cradled in her arms and against her muscular body. She lowered Charlie onto her cock, back in control again.

The position was new and thrilling to Charlie. Kal was demonstrating her superior strength as a mortal god by holding her lover's weight. She gasped when the thick cock pushed through her entrance and filled her again. She moaned and rested her head against Kal's shoulder. Each time Kal lifted her and lowered her onto her cock, Charlie became needier. Her soaking inner walls hugged every inch of cock that Kal gave her, but the rhythm was painstaking. Charlie squeezed her own breast, rolling the hard nipple between her fingers.

With a turn of her head, Charlie tasted Kal's skin for the first time, kissing her neck. She grinned when she received a low, pleased rumble. She tested Kal's tolerance further and pressed her lips against the hot skin. This time she licked with the flat of her tongue, tasting the wonderful spicy scent. Past lovers paled compared to Kal. How could someone be this desirable?

Charlie expected a warning from an Alpha for going near the neck. Instead, Kal tilted her head to one side in silent offer. She stared at the expanse of the neck, eyeing a delicate vein. Charlie kissed the spot and grazed her teeth, but never bit. From rumors, she knew it was safer not to bite an Alpha unless she wanted to fight for dominance again.

At first, Kal's thunderous vibration sounded dangerous, but they held blissful. She returned her focus to pleasing Charlie on her cock again but at a brutally slow pace, as if memorizing the silky depth of Charlie's pussy.

Close to madness, Charlie craned her neck and raked her teeth over Kal's pulse point behind her jaw. It was a risky move that she explained with a needy plea in Kalmarese. "*Krafka.*" She threaded her fingers into dark strands of hair and murmured, "I need you to fuck m-me." Her voice quaked and cracked on the last syllable.

After a few heartbeats, worry niggled at Charlie until Kal snarled like a wolf. She lifted Charlie off her cock and placed her flat against the bed. The air was knocked from Charlie's chest, but she had little time to balk at the roughness even if it excited her. Her legs were thrown over Kal's shoulders and before she could lift her head, Kal was back inside her. "*Vuk!*" She raised her ass, meeting the next thrust with eager demand.

Kal clamped her palms around Charlie's calves, then snapped her hips back before driving in again. Charlie yelped and clenched her teeth at first. But the pounding became rough and hot, more than meeting her earlier request. "Gods! *Ja!*" Charlie latched onto the bed while her lover fucked her pussy. The loud wet slaps matched the hammering of her heart. "S-so fucking g-good!" Above her, Kal grunted and growled between plunges.

The building heat in Charlie's gut made her bow her back. She took everything Kal gave her and hoped her pussy's tightness felt amazing for her lover. From the uncontrollable thrusts, Kal seemed uncaged and determined to break Charlie open. Charlie sensed the initial spark, causing her to tense. Kal's next stroke was slower but deliciously deep, driving Charlie over the ledge. Her eyes rolled back when the passion consumed her. For a beat, she was certain she heard Kal cry out. Charlie's walls fluttered, then clenched around Kal, holding them together. A warm fluid filled her further, and they moaned in unison.

With a hand against her heaving chest, Charlie attempted to fathom how Kal could fuck her so well. She had slept with many lovers in her lifetime and believed a few of them were skillful. She'd been wrong. Kal had raised Charlie's standards of an amazing fuck. Placing her other hand against her lower belly, she pressed down and groaned from the sensation of Kal's cock buried in her.

She stretched her arm further and touched the exposed length outside of her pussy.

"Damn," she muttered and dropped back against the bed.

Kal ran her hands along Charlie's legs, closer to her knees. She massaged the muscle and skin there. "You are far too concerned about how much you can take." With a soft roll of her hips, she rubbed her cockhead and girth against Charlie's walls.

Charlie half groaned and whimpered. She regained her voice after Kal went still. "Compatibility issues." She wondered if she could handle more if they practiced more. They would never know since this was their one night. After a deep breath, she asked, "Am I still too tight?"

"*Ja.*"

Charlie sighed at her body's betrayal, her inner muscles holding on to Kal's cock as if it were a prize to keep. "*Krafka.* Give me another moment." She nibbled on her bottom lip and decided to tease Kal. "You are big." Even though she couldn't see Kal's smirk, she heard it in the low rumble rolling around deep in Kal's chest. Somehow she suspected being locked together was a compliment to Kal. After all, Alphas formed a ring at the base of their cock during a rut and knotted their mate.

For a moment, there was silence between them that was both peaceful and comforting, compared to the start of their relationship. On the first day, Kal had been a dark force on the throne that had willed Charlie to kneel to her. Although tonight she held the command in their relationship, it was an arrangement rather than a forced situation. But Charlie found an underlying comfort in surrendering to Kal, who had met her needs without hesitation.

Charlie *was* safe with Kal.

Uneasy about the realization, Charlie focused on the present and their current tie. "Can you try now?"

Kal cupped the underside of Charlie's ass and gently pulled her hips away. She paused when Charlie groaned, and raised an eyebrow. Charlie promised she was fine, so Kal continued to withdraw. Once separated, Kal dropped to the bed next to Charlie and held her cock at the base.

Charlie sneaked a glance and smirked at the softness of the shaft in Kal's hand. But her gut instinct told her it would be short-lived. Kal was an Alpha after all, and many were familiar with their stamina. Already a tingle danced along Charlie's spine at the thought of a long night together. She closed her eyes and allowed herself to doze off, assuming Kal would stir her when it was time for more.

Chapter 6

Charlie released a groan and turned onto her right side, enjoying the comfort around her. A light but cool breeze brushed across her cheek, making her grumble and burrow under the heavy cover. As she settled again, her mind continued stirring awake, and the warm scent near her played with her memories. She remembered coming over to Kal's room, stripping off their clothes, and then fucking through most of the night.

She jolted awake, concerned about staying overnight in Kal's bed. Her racing heart made her scan the nearby space, which was the bed's messy and empty landscape. The familiar spice that was Kal lingered, meaning she might be sleeping beside Charlie. But, no, Kal was missing, and Charlie was concerned about what could happen next. Based on the sunshine in the room, it was the morning after; Charlie recalled a few too many awkward mornings in her past sexual encounters.

After she sat up, another soft breeze touched her flushed skin. The source seemed to be from behind a sheer drape that fluttered in the air from the light wind off a balcony. An outline of a figure's back stood out against the drape.

Clenching her lip between her teeth, Charlie considered what to do and scanned for her clothes. They were folded on the long bench near the doorway between the bedroom and sitting room. She muttered a curse when she realized it was unwise to put them on when she smelled like sex and Alpha. Another Kalmar would figure them out in two ticks or faster. However, her attention shifted to the black robe that was resting on her side of the bed at the foot. It was an invitation, so she slid out of the bed and put on the cool, soft attire. After tying it, Charlie headed to the balcony and did her best to not trip on the robe due to its length.

Beside the floating drape, Charlie made out Kal's distant features and offered, "Good morning." Unsure how to handle their unusual situation, she remained positioned near the drape so it hid her from the city and any onlookers but kept her in Kal's view.

Kal turned her attention to her human lover and returned the greeting.

In a heartbeat, Charlie sensed a different aura from Kal. She shifted from foot to foot and crossed her arms.

She reminded herself not to overthink last night's choices, which they both made as adults. Charlie had accepted both the decision and the potential circumstance if word spread about her and Kal, a human and a Kalmar.

Clearing her throat, Charlie mentioned, "I'll grab my stuff and—"

"Stand out here with me," Kal ordered.

Charlie swallowed first but agreed and stepped out onto the balcony beside Kal. As she took in the beautiful view of Tarrak, her concerns faded away, leaving her with a thin smile. From so high up, it would be impossible for anyone to see them together, and this eased her nerves.

"Beautiful, is it not?"

"*Ja*," Charlie whispered.

From the fifty-first floor of the Great Tower, the city's buildings and people were painted across the lands until they faded away against the farmland in the distance. To the right was the Koblenz River with wooden ships that sailed, motored, or moved by oar power. A gull's familiar cry traveled across the winds and made it to their ears. Despite the cool day, the sunlight was soothing against Charlie's face.

"You came to my planet at what age?" Kal asked, but her attention remained on the city.

Returning to the present, Charlie sighed and answered, "I was about seven when the *Liberator* made it here." She was well aware of Kal's possession of Kander, fitting into the role of god to this world. However, there was no arrogance in Kal's claim over Kander.

"When did you leave?"

The difficult memories drifted back to Charlie. She had started a new stage of her life that shaped her into the mercenary she was today. "Fourteen." Two days after her birthday, she ran away from the adoptive family who raised her on Kander and started her new life.

Kal hummed low until it deepened into a rumble. "Will you ever settle down again?"

Charlie snorted and glanced at Kal before saying, "People in my line of work don't exactly retire." She gazed out at the city and whispered, "We simply go out with a bang."

A comfortable quietness lingered between them, both basking in the gorgeous lands and lost in thought. For a moment, Charlie was taken back to Earth and was reminded why planets like Kander were so special. One of her last memories on Earth was hiking through a national park and enjoying the sunny day, birds flying overhead, squirrels racing across the trail, and sounds of a nearby creek's soft babble. She let out a heavy breath and wished that Earth had survived the interstellar war, but its destruction had saved the Milky Way, for now.

"What became of your family?"

Charlie frowned and wondered why they were circling back to her family history. Perhaps it was the simple fact Kal had forgotten her own or couldn't remember due to her ascension as a god-ruler. "They died on Earth when it was blown up."

"Brothers or sisters?"

After a huff, Charlie shook her head and explained, "*Joh.* I was pretty much born in a lab." She tightened her arms and swallowed against the faint lump in her throat. "My biological mother and father were donors because my legal parents couldn't get pregnant. But my legal mother did carry me to term… almost." She was born months early and started her life in a plastic box at a hospital. At least, she'd heard her family talk about her birth on occasion. At the time, she was a kid and sometimes the adult chatter was boring. Today, she couldn't ask her parents how she was conceived and born.

Again Kal was silent, seeming to take in Charlie's turbulent life. "Did you meet your biological parents?"

"*Joh*, it was a closed deal." Charlie shrugged, then whispered, "Maybe I would have searched for them when I was old enough." She flashed a smirk at Kal. "Doesn't matter now that we blew Earth the fuck up." She tilted her head and asked, "What about you and your family?" She watched for any hint of an expression on Kal's face, trying to find some scrap of emotion rather than the firm armor.

"My people are my family," Kal stated.

Charlie dragged her fingers through her messy hair and grumbled at how the answer was rote in nature. She blew out a low breath, debating whether to test the waters between them. "I know the stories that Kal, the High Commander, carries Kalatas inside them, but you were born like any Kalmar. You had to have parents." She shook her head and asked, "Don't you remember? Or did you choose to forget?" Some part of her ached for Kal no matter the answer. The idea that somebody had to lose their identity to serve a calling was both honorable and horrifying to her. As the beats stretched on, she was uncertain Kal would even humor her.

But then Kal regarded Charlie, and behind her bright green eyes was a slight spark. "My oldest memory is looking into the Light of Kalatas, then it fading away, and I was seated upon the throne in front of my people.

Whatever my life had been before that moment was meaningless to what I saw in the Light of Kalatas. I am filled with all the knowledge of the past Kals and the Spirit of Kalatas." She held Charlie's stare with conviction and added, "You would understand if you could gaze into the Light."

Charlie shook her head, and a low heat burned under her skin. "But you are more than just a god." She held out her hand at the city and river in front of them. "You came from a home out there with a family. You probably had friends. A house you were born in. Maybe you rode a horse as a kid. Maybe you broke your arm when you were nine. Or maybe you had feelings for the Omega who lived next door. Or or or…" She crossed her arms again and huffed at the distant look on Kal's face, but there was something else that she couldn't read.

"Sometimes…" Kal hesitated for the first time but pressed forward with a faint shake behind her words. "Sometimes fragments come back like a ghost." She pursed her lips and further confessed, "Each time I try to hold on to them too hard, they vanish." With a sigh, she looked at Charlie and stated, "I am not meant to remember my mortal life."

"Until your death," Charlie whispered, her heart growing heavy. She was split in half, both disliking and revering the god of Kander. This Kal, whoever she was, had made the ultimate sacrifice for her people. Their god, Kalatas, had no qualms with taking a body and wiping out her individuality. All High Commanders were a vessel for the god. However, in the end, Kalatas cared for its people and planet, taking action rather than being a passive god. Perhaps Earth would still exist if its god had intervened and halted doomsday.

Bowing her head, Charlie whispered, "It's not my place to give such a damn but…" She met Kal's hard stare. "Taking away what makes you an individual is not fair."

Kal revealed a dark smile and shifted closer. "Every Alpha who has looked into the Light of Kalatas has done so willingly and with a sense of duty." She grew serious, and a rumble filled her chest. "Even you should be able to respect my choice to make this sacrifice for my people."

Charlie deduced arguing further about it was a dangerous idea. There were better reasons than this to intentionally provoke Kal's Alpha. She gave a nod and promised, "I do respect your choice more than you probably know." Defusing the situation altogether, she said, "I should get ready and go."

"It is wise that you bathe before you put on your clothes."

Dragging her fingers through her messy hair, Charlie bit her bottom lip and conceded with Kal. She followed Kal into the bathroom that was the size of Charlie's own room. With a slack jaw, she took in the local decor such as old crossed swords hanging under twin windows high up and a scenic countryside mural painted on the entire left wall. In the left corner was a walk-in shower. And in the center was a gigantic stone tub that commanded all the attention. The damn thing could easily hold four people.

Kal went around it and worked a few knobs that released hot water into the nearly full tub. Fresh steam wafted through the room. Charlie suspected that Kal had turned on the water earlier this morning in preparation for their bath. Her heart lurched at the idea that they were bathing together in daylight. Last night had been easier when they could mask themselves under the dim candlelight.

Undeterred by the situation, Kal freed the robe's tie as she approached the stone steps that led up to the tub. Her robe fell and cascaded away from her body, exposing her bronzy skin and black mane. With grace, she descended into the inviting water that was giving off a flowery scent and sat down with her back against the tub's wall.

After a deep breath, Charlie grappled with her natural reaction to Kal's beauty and power, but it was useless. She grumbled at herself and decided, for now, to accept how her body wanted Kal so much. Her trembling hands made it difficult to free the robe's sash, but Charlie pushed it off her shoulders and ascended the steps. She felt Kal's eyes on her, burning into every centimeter of her skin. Charlie was beginning to realize their fiery attraction was mutual, even if it was considered unnatural among their people.

The tub was indeed large and luxurious. Charlie took a seat to Kal's right, close but never touching. For a moment, she enjoyed the hot water that soothed sore muscles throughout her body, especially ones that had been worked so well last night. She released a contented sigh, closed her eyes, and leaned her head against the tub. Already, desire started to brew between them again.

"Has every Kal been an Alpha?"

"All but the first." Kal shifted, which caused water to move. "Only an Omega can give birth and nurture the people."

Charlie had heard a different history and mythology about previous High Commanders, but she found it more interesting to learn from a High Commander. Few humans had an opportunity like she did now.

"There is a prophecy that if Kal is an Omega again, it will be the end of days."

Cracking open an eye, Charlie spied the seriousness on Kal's face. Such dark folklore made Charlie straighten and open both eyes. "In human religion, Omega always meant the end. Our god was the Alpha and the Omega, which meant the beginning and the end." She noticed Kal was quite interested in the information.

"Perhaps our gods were related, then."

Charlie huffed and argued, "I hope not, for Kander's sake." A dark coil unfurled inside her as she thought about what happened to Earth. "When the Sworne came to our solar system, to our planet, our god did nothing. He remained silent and hidden and left us to fight alone." She gritted her teeth and started to shake.

"We blew up Earth to save the rest of the galaxy, and nobody gives a fucking rat's ass, much less thanks us."

Kal was quiet, then pushed off the wall, nearing Charlie. "I admire your people and especially your spirit to fight." She paused in front of Charlie, though never touching bodies. "Your people are safe here on Kander." Her declaration echoed her promise from last night about Charlie's safety.

Charlie believed Kal.

After cooling her emotions, Charlie nodded, then glanced away and tried reminding herself that she shouldn't give a damn about what happened to Earthlings. "No planet is safe with the Sworne out there."

Thunder rolled through Kal's chest before she stated, "Perhaps the Sworne will fear Kander now that the rebel Earthlings are here."

Despite the conversation, Charlie couldn't help a small laugh at the joke, but then maybe Kal had a point. Still, if the Sworne learned of Kander's resources and darakar, it would be the beginning of the end. She doubted it would be this lifetime or even the next, but soon a High Commander would battle the Sworne. Some piece of Charlie wanted to see the face-off even if she already knew the story's ending.

A light touch to Charlie's thigh made her refocus on Kal. As they held each other's eyes, she knew what was to come between them. Often there would be foreplay, seducing, or even a bit of kissing, but Kal was an Alpha and a Kalmar, both known for getting straight to the point. Still, she wanted to ease into their next fuck.

"Have you ever been with a human before?" Charlie asked, nudging the conversation back to personal topics. Nothing was given away in Kal's features, but she saw Kal's pupils dilate. She fought back the temptation to drift into waiting hands.

"*Joh.*"

The answer was clipped and firm but filled Charlie with a sense of relief and a bit of pride that she was Kal's first. She held down on her smirk, not wanting to incite Kal's Alpha. However, a piece of her wondered if Kal chose her because she was safe, and so that no other Kalmar learned their ruler had an affinity for humans. Soon Charlie would return to space and be off Kander, leaving no evidence of their forbidden affair.

"Have you been with a Kalmar?"

Kal's rumbly voice recalled Charlie. How she loved the heaviness of Kal's voice that held an animalistic note to it. Charlie melted under it, then her clit throbbed.

Clenching her hand under the water, she whispered, "You're my first." The slight curl of Kal's lips sent a charge through Charlie.

"I am a special breed of Alpha called a Carnec. We are a blend of both Alpha and Omega." Kal tilted her head, studying Charlie. "Did you know of Carnec Alphas before me?"

"*J-J*—" Charlie cleared her throat and cursed the burn in her cheeks. "*Joh*."

"We are extremely rare," Kal explained. "Some are even killed at birth."

Charlie was distraught by the information even though she'd grown up around the Kalmar's harsh ways. "Why?" The idea that any intelligent race would kill their young was horrific.

"There are some that see a Carnec Alpha as a mistake of nature."

"But are there Carnec Omegas too? Do they kill them?"

"*Ja*, there are Carnec Omegas." After a low hum, Kal lowered her attention to the steaming water and replied, "Omegas are generally prized, so even a Carnec Omega can have a place."

Disturbed by the history behind Carnec Alphas, Charlie wished to learn more about Kal's own past and why her family kept her alive, even though such questions would always remain unanswered. Frowning a little, she said, "I guess you get why the hybrids feared the Degenerate Kill Order."

Bowing her head, Kal whispered, "*Ja*." Her dark stare was centered on Charlie, as if there was nothing else that mattered on the planet. Kal returned to her earlier spot, her back pressing against the tub's wall. "Perhaps you would like to learn more about a Carnec Alpha." She placed her hands on top of the tub's side, lifting her body up from the water.

Kal's rare but sexy smile caused Charlie's heart to jump to light speed. She did her best to appear calm. Before even getting a single word out, she watched Kal starting to rise from the steamy water.

Charlie's eyes traveled down Kal's neck until her view was filled by the round breasts and hard nipples. The water continued running down Kal's tan skin and twisted across the defined stomach muscles before pooling between her muscular legs and dripping off the end of her cock. Kal slid her ass onto the top of the tub, leaving herself on full display for Charlie's hungry eyes.

With a quickened pulse, Charlie was certain her heart would break through her chest. She managed to breathe and hold a slight poker face even while her stomach quivered over and over. She was confused why her natural response toward Kal's nudity was to lose her senses. Maybe Kal casted a spell on her, or maybe it was a trance. Kal held out a hand, beckoning Charlie to her.

Charlie crossed the steamy expanse between them and stood beside Kal, her nipples brushing against a thigh. In the daylight, she had a gorgeous view of what made Kal a rare Carnec Alpha. Between two muscular legs was the long, thick length that had both pleased and fucked her last night, making her scream and orgasm. A moan broke free from her lips, and she regretted it until Kal's soft growl made a dull, needy ache start low in her gut. Then she was forced to clench her teeth when Kal grabbed her cock.

A few times, Kal stroked the length and rubbed her thumb across the soaked tip. She moaned, then looked at Charlie. "Do you wish to touch me?"

Charlie bobbed her head and managed to find her voice again. "*Ja*."

From her higher position, Kal smirked at her lover and shifted until her right leg was deeper in the water and her left foot was against the top of the tub. She gave Charlie better access and withdrew her hand, showing off the hardness of her cock.

Charlie had touched Kal the past evening, but it was brief and in the dark. A clear fluid beaded at the cock's reddened tip. Kal had ejaculated last night but informed Charlie she could only impregnate her lover during a rut. For a tick, her eyes drifted down to the base of Kal's cock and noticed a soft bump. She knew it was the knot that would enlarge during a rut and forever bind Kal to one mate. She envied whoever would have that pleasure one day, if anyone.

After taking a steady breath, Charlie pressed her palm against the firm shaft, halfway between the tip and the base. As her fingers wrapped around the length, she realized how much she enjoyed last night and hated their limited time together. Somehow, that worried her, and a desperate voice in her head urged her to have sex one last time with Kal.

"You do not have to be so gentle." Kal's voice was thick and heady near Charlie's ear. She growled low when Charlie's grip increased against her cock. "Better." She leaned into Charlie's space, breathing in her scent.

Charlie drew her hand down, near the base, and ran her thumb across the faint knot that was a ring around Kal's cock. "Can you get pregnant?" If Kal was both an Alpha and an Omega, then it should be possible.

Chuckling, Kal brushed her lips along Charlie's jawline until she was near a soft ear draped by golden strands. "*Ja*," she murmured. "But I am better at giving than receiving."

Charlie's mind went in several directions after learning that a Carnec Alpha had both reproductive organs from an Alpha and an Omega. She was tempted to lower her hand past the cock's base, wanting to find out if there was a vaginal opening. But an unexpected nip against her throat made her clench Kal's cock harder. A snarl filled her ear and caused her stomach to tremble while her clit pulsed hard. The building need to have Kal inside her became priority. She returned to the cockhead and massaged it with her thumb, earning a growly moan.

Kal then trembled when Charlie tugged on her cock. She bared her teeth at Charlie before saying, "The tip is sensitive."

Charlie returned to the head and tested Kal's response. She grinned at how her lover jolted and curled her fingers around the tub. The head seemed to be as sensitive as Charlie's clitoris. Gently, she circled the pad of her thumb over the tip, using the fluid to her advantage. Kal clenched her teeth and growled more and more. She lifted her ass off the side, meeting Charlie's touch.

But Charlie withdrew her thumb and was overtaken with the desire to taste Kal. She'd given oral sex to another female human, who was a mercenary too. They'd met on Lerto and stumbled back to Charlie's quarters on the *Pacifica.* Never had she entertained, much less wanted to suck on any cock, especially one of Kal's size. Yet she was driven with pure desire, lowering her head until Kal halted her.

"*Joh,*" Kal ordered, and blackness swirled in her eyes when Charlie looked at her.

Biting on a curse, Charlie recalled that the Kalmar weren't interested in anything oral. Or at least those were the stories told around the tables at the Earthling settlement in Kander. She straightened and held Kal's gaze, waiting for their next move. She continued to massage the shaft in hopes to save their time together.

Kal leaned in again, using her scent to entice Charlie. "Do you want me to fuck you again?"

After a deep inhale, Charlie tugged on Kal's cock and confessed, "I need you to." She was startled when Kal slid into the tub and grabbed her, causing her to yelp. She was forced to turn around and bend over the side. She was flush with need to have Kal in her again. Then the flared head nudged her entrance, testing and teasing her.

"Is this what you want?" Kal secured one hand at Charlie's waist, then rolled her hips and played with Charlie.

"*Ja,*" Charlie admitted aloud. Yesterday she would have denied ever wanting to be with a Kalmar Alpha. But Kal was so enticing, beautiful, and dark that it pulled at a cord in Charlie, which scared her deeper still. As Kal's cock pushed past her entrance, she forgot her fears and became lost in the sweet stretch inside her.

Kal continued easing into Charlie. Her growl was thick with passion and shook deep in her chest. She held on to Charlie with both hands and halted when she reached Charlie's limit. Leaning forward, she pressed her front against Charlie's back, her hard nipples brushing against hot skin.

For a brief instant, Charlie stared up at the painting that covered the wall from end to end and top to bottom. It reminded her of the countryside on Earth, but she knew it was a painting of Kander's landscape. Her eyes then screwed shut when Kal pulled out a little then pushed in, again and again.

Kal stroked Charlie's tight walls with slow, deliberate movements of her hips. Her grunts mixed with Charlie's sweet moans.

"*Vuk*," Charlie murmured and groaned. "It feels so good." Somehow it was better than last night, and maybe her body had adjusted to Kal's size better. The initial sting was gone, and it encouraged her to move with Kal's motions. "You feel so good in me."

Kal snarled in response, then drove forward and pinned Charlie against the tub with her weight. She bowed her head, teeth grazing across flushed skin, and she whispered, "You smell sweeter than any Omega." Her confession revealed what Charlie suspected earlier.

"Are you completely in me?" Charlie knew the answer despite the fact she hoped otherwise. Her mild disappointment was fractured by Kal's soft laugh.

"So concerned about how much of my cock is in you." Kal had a point. It was a bit unbelievable that a human was hyperfocused on taking one's cock rather than the Alpha.

Deep inside, Charlie wanted her lover to be as satisfied as she was. With a cant of her head, she tried stealing a glance at Kal. "I want it all," she revealed in a half truth, unable to voice her secret. She watched Kal's Alpha ego inflate with the lift of her chest. "Can you blame me?"

Kal rolled her hips and bared her teeth when Charlie whimpered under her. "You are taking more in than last night." She bit Charlie's ear, then whispered, "You must want it all."

Charlie's eyes fluttered. She lost the battle to withhold more of the truth, which spilled from her lips. "I've never felt this." She both heard and felt Kal's thick purr that soothed her own internal struggle with their unusual circumstance.

"You will not again," Kal said, grunting low, then lifting herself off Charlie. She pulled her hips back farther, then pumped back into Charlie, who hissed low. "Ever," she declared in a strong voice. She adjusted their position and started to take Charlie. Her girthy length pushed through Charlie's tight walls. After a minute, she increased the pace, eliciting louder yells from Charlie.

Every plunge stole Charlie's breath and sent searing heat rippling through her. Charlie needed more. She dragged her nails against the stone, holding on during the rough fucking. But then it all ended before she could climax. Her breath hitched while her body trembled in place. She tried to turn but Kal's firm hand on her back halted her.

"The guards are at the door again. If you become any louder, I will have to stop." Kal warned Charlie with a deep thrust back inside. "Do not make me stop."

"Gag me if you have to, but don't you dare stop," Charlie demanded. If she had known sooner, she would have used her techbit to set up a sound barrier.

Kal taunted her lover with a soft rock of her hips and earned a moan from Charlie. "I would rather not gag you." She returned to the earlier pace, thrusting and clawing against Charlie. She slipped a hand between Charlie's legs and dipped her fingers into silky wetness.

"*Vuuuuk*," Charlie rasped when Kal started rubbing her swollen clitoris too. She clenched her teeth and held down her yells but a few whimpers spilled out. Her inner walls clenched and shuddered against the throbbing cock that hit her core. A soft sting started behind her eyes, and she felt the hot pressure start to overwhelm her. She was close and rocked back on Kal.

A guttural sound erupted from Kal as she plunged back in. Charlie's slick walls spasmed and locked around her cock, clenching and demanding of her. Like Charlie, she slid down until she caught them both with a hand on the tub's side. With a grunt, Kal hooked her arms around Charlie, then hauled them up, bodies molded together. She nudged her cock inside Charlie, who whined and clenched her lover's muscular arms. Kal buried her face near Charlie's head, her teeth grazing delicate flesh but never breaking skin.

Weakened by the orgasm and a good fuck, Charlie relied on Kal to keep her standing until she could find her strength again. While she regained her senses, Kal grounded her with low rumbles. Deep in her, Kal's length remained buried and filled her with a warm comfort. The lightheadedness faded and the afterglow remained under her skin. Their connection was more than a physical one, but Charlie was unwilling to explore it more. They walked different paths and were from different worlds.

Seeming to sense Charlie's thoughts, Kal bent her knees, inched out a bit of her cock, and then ordered, "Lean over the tub."

Once free of Kal's thick arms, Charlie leaned over the side again and took a deep breath, which further relaxed her body. Kal withdrew from her, and she moaned in disappointment. Behind her, she heard the water move, so she turned and found Kal against the tub's wall. Charlie sank into the steamy water. From across the tub, she felt a hungry stare, but she chose to shut her eyes, knowing they'd never leave the room if this kept going between them.

After a few minutes, Kal moved and prompted Charlie to watch her lover bath. There was a selection of different bars on a wooden tray. Kal cleaned her hair with one, then used a different one for her body. She came over to Charlie and handed her the first bar, which had a rustic scent to it. "Finish getting ready while I retrieve your guard." After she deposited the soap into Charlie's small hand, Kal went to the steps and ascended them.

Holding her breath, Charlie gaped at the gorgeous Alpha body that left the tub. "Damn," she muttered. Kal might have ruined Charlie for any new lovers. After a sigh, she cleaned herself with the different soaps and exited the bath. Kal was long gone, but a towel had been left on the counter for her. Once dried, Charlie deposited the towel and entered the bedroom when Kal returned from the sitting room. Kal was dressed while Charlie wore only an awkward smile.

"Your guard will be here shortly," Kal informed in a businesslike tone.

Charlie pursed her lips and murmured, "Right." She went over to her clothes on the bench and readied herself before the Omega guard came for her. Behind her, she heard movements around the room and even metal tapping against metal. Once clothed, Charlie jammed her feet into the boots and sat down on the bench to lace them. Kal returned from the bathroom when Charlie stood. They were both dressed in their normal attire as if last night were a dream.

"What about the other guards?" Charlie asked.

"I dismissed them," Kal explained and escorted Charlie to the double doors.

Charlie paused beside the sealed doors and turned to Kal. "My guard is an Omega. I didn't think there were any soldiers that were Omegas."

A deep hum shook in Kal's chest before she reminded, "Much has changed since your last time here."

"*Ja*, I haven't been receiving the Kander newsletters in my inbox," Charlie joked and dragged her fingers through her damp hair. She'd blow dry it later, but at least she didn't carry Kal's scent. "What's the Omega's name?"

"Andren."

"Andren," Charlie repeated and smiled. She should have asked the guard herself, but she couldn't bring herself to chat with Andren. A Kalmar soldier, who was a guard and an Omega was more intimidating than an Alpha. For an Omega to enter the Alpha-dominated army, she had to be strong-willed and determined.

Kal shifted closer but never allowed them to touch, knowing the consequences. "Come to my office at the fourteenth hour."

Narrowing her eyes, Charlie weighed the order, which held an undertone of request to it. They weren't going to have sex again, so it had to be business related. She nodded, then toyed with the buckle at her waist. She recalled the Kalmarese word for thanking someone and gathered her courage to say it. "*Tah.*" After a swallow, she straightened her shoulders and added, "For last night." She cleared her throat when Kal raised an eyebrow at her.

Bending forward, Kal brushed her lips near Charlie's ear and teased, "Put it toward your fee for returning the Omega." Her banter was unexpected, but it created a thin crack in Charlie's wall.

Playing along, Charlie smirked and joked, "I'll consider it a sign-on bonus." She shivered when her lover backed off, leaving her distinct scent under Charlie's nose.

A primal part of Charlie wanted to bask in Kal's special scent.

Fuck. I need to get out of here, she told herself.

Kal yanked the door open and revealed the Omega guard, Andren, waiting in the hallway. As Charlie passed her, she whispered, "*Tah*, too, for last night."

Startled, Charlie pivoted back in Kal's direction, but she paused halfway and refrained from a foolish action in front of Andren. She offered a smile at Kal, who had a faint glow to her eyes. There was a subtle shift in Kal that was too much for Charlie. She turned away and hastened toward Andren.

"See that she eats," Kal ordered Andren in her rumbly voice.

"*Ja*, Kal," Andren replied and started for the open elevator.

Charlie followed and stood next to Andren in the lift, which moved after Andren closed the gate. Today's plans formulated in her head; it would be a busy day. Before eating, she would catch up with her crew and make sure they were okay. Starr might have paced a hole into the bedroom's floor by now. After a heavy sigh, she glanced over and narrowed her eyes at the smirk on Andren's face.

"If you say a word," Charlie threatened, "I will launch you into outer space myself, Andren." She shook with silent laughter when Andren went from smug to pure shock in one tick. Satisfied that Andren understood her, she slid open the gate for them.

Andren went out first, ever the guard, but paused at the opening and argued, "Why do you think Kal chose me as your guard?"

Chapter 7

Charlie hurried out of the elevator and left Andren scrambling after her. She knew the way to Kal's office and sensed she was close to being late, again. She cursed herself for getting distracted with the walk through the city with Starr, but they both had needed the fresh air to clear their heads. Even if time was longer on Kander than on Earth, it somehow still managed to get away from Charlie.

Andren puffed when they paused in front of the guarded doors to the office. "Kal is expecting the merc."

Charlie rolled her eyes at how every Kalmar refused to use her name, as if it were a sin.

One guard knocked on the door, warning the High Commander first, then poking his head in to receive muffled orders. He turned back to Charlie and signaled for her to enter the office. Kal was coming from the sofa and instructed Andren to remain outside with the others. Once the door shut, she lowered her attention to Charlie but remained quiet.

A tremble passed through Charlie, yet she held Kal's intense gaze, never breaking under it. As she parted her lips, she caught movement behind Kal and reached for her confiscated gun and cursed. However, Kal seemed at ease, which made Charlie relax.

"There is somebody who wishes to see you," Kal explained and stepped aside as the second person approached.

With a furrow stretched across her brow, Charlie cut her eyes to the newcomer and lost control of her jaw. "By all the gods of the galaxy," she whispered in awe.

"*Turen*, Charlie."

After the warm hello, Charlie rushed across the short distance and enveloped Dorlon into the biggest hug. When Dorlon chuckled, she laughed back and tightened her arms. "It's so good to see you after so long." She forced herself to withdraw, yet her hands remained on her friend's padded shoulders.

"You too, my friend." Dorlon was taller than Charlie and had the most beautiful brown eyes. She had grown into adulthood well, even bulkier than Charlie would expect of an Omega. She once had long light-colored hair, but it was now shoulder length and framed her round features.

Charlie released Dorlon, then was punched hard in the shoulder. She hissed, bent forward, and clutched her injury, glaring at her old friend. Everyone from her past seemed to have the same reaction.

"That's for leaving without a goodbye."

"Goddamn it, Dorlon." Charlie glowered and rubbed the spot a few more times. She deserved it, along with plenty more. Leaving Kander meant she abandoned Dorlon and Raine, her two best friends at the time.

"I should give you one for every year." Dorlon folded her arms and gave Charlie a glare.

Rolling her shoulder, Charlie shook her head and was tongue-tied while she took in Dorlon, who stood with a rigid posture. Dorlon's punch had bite to it compared to how they used to wrestle. Dorlon was dressed like a warrior with two laser guns on her hips and a sword hilt protruding past her head. After a confused headshake, Charlie stated, "You're a soldier."

"Dorlon is one of my commanders," Kal cut in, reminding Charlie that she was there. Pride lingered in her gaze. "She is the commander of the Kardos province."

"Wow," Charlie whispered, then smiled at Dorlon. "You went from drowning in a river to commanding the province." Her smile shifted into a grin when Dorlon cracked her own smirk, but Dorlon turned serious toward the High Commander.

As if sensing the situation, Kal huffed low and exchanged a silent agreement with Dorlon before she turned to Charlie. "I must attend to a few things. You both may remain here to visit."

"*Tah*, Kal."

Before Charlie could offer her appreciation too, Kal was gone from the room. Did Kal go out of her way to set up the reunion between her and Dorlon? Kardos was far from Tarrak, so their meeting wasn't by chance. The gesture softened her opinion about the stoic ruler. She sighed, then teased, "So how have you been, Commander Dorlon?"

Dorlon rolled her eyes and said, "Sit down with me." She returned to the sofa and remained quiet once Charlie sat beside her. As a pup, she had been withdrawn and cautious. Today she held a confident air that made Charlie wonder if this was the same person.

"You look good," Charlie commented first.

"So do you."

Charlie chuckled and sank into the comfortable sofa, still wrapping her mind around the fact that Dorlon was here. "Space has been kinder than last time." Her friend had heard many stories from her and Raine about their time on the *Liberator.*

"I thought you had enough of that damn place."

After a shrug, Charlie argued, "You know I've always loved the stars."

Dorlon grunted, then dragged her fingers through her hair. She placed an arm on top of the sofa and studied Charlie, as if also grasping that their visit was real. They had spent years of their youth together and formed a special bond. Back then, they may have been the only human and Kalmar to befriend each other. Later, Raine entered their circle, adding more depth to their friendship.

"*Tah* for the job, by the way." Charlie tilted her head, then asked, "How did you know I was a merc?"

"We still get space traders in Kardos, and your name has traveled across the galaxy." Dorlon indicated Charlie's features. "A blond-haired human merc with a mouth doesn't go unnoticed anywhere."

Charlie snorted at the smart remark. She crossed her legs and recalled her old nickname from childhood. "I'm hardly Chatty Charlie anymore." They had taught each other their native languages, dying to talk and connect.

"I find that hard to believe," Dorlon debated.

Early on in their friendship, Charlie didn't stop speaking in English to Dorlon, who couldn't understand her. However, Charlie's persistence won Dorlon over, and a tentative tolerance started between them. The memories were distant and seemed like another life. Charlie had changed since then.

"How is your brother Alsace?" Charlie had never met him, but she cared about him. Alsace had done his best to protect Dorlon from their abusive father. Charlie respected Alsace for it.

"He is well." Dorlon smiled, warm and gentle. "I'm an aunt now."

Charlie mirrored the smile and pictured pups jumping around their Aunt Dorlon, vying for attention. "Mated then?" After Dorlon's nod, she considered the one other family member in Dorlon's life. "And your sire?"

Dorlon looked away and shifted before she regarded Charlie again. "Dead." The hardness in her voice sent a chill down Charlie's spine. "The drinking caught up to him." Whether his death was the alcohol itself or a related cause was hard to say. Charlie also didn't care, relieved he was out of Dorlon's life.

"How did you become the commander of Kardos?" Charlie hoped the new topic redirected Dorlon's thoughts.

"Kal asked." Dorlon offered no other details. She was always reserved, but now she was guarded too. Charlie could *see* the hardened mask Dorlon wore compared to her openness when they were kids. Dorlon had been chosen over an Alpha to be the commander, and with excellent reason.

"You mentored Kal."

"I did," Dorlon agreed. Again her simple answer blocked Charlie.

After an exhale, Charlie continued to push the conversation in hopes to find her old friend inside Dorlon. "How long have you known each other?" Part of her considered whether Dorlon might know who Kal was before the ascension to power.

"About fourteen years now."

Charlie resisted the urge to grab Dorlon, unsure how comfortable Dorlon was with physical contact. They might have hugged, but a punch followed it. "So you knew her before she was Kal?"

"*Ja.* I trained her before and after her ascension." Dorlon tilted her head, but there was a slight glint of warning in her eyes. "But who she was is long gone and replaced by Kalatas."

Charlie shook her head at how her old friend could still read her mind. She nibbled on her lip and asked, "How do you like being a commander?"

Dorlon grinned and admitted, "It's not what I imagined doing with my life, but I love it."

"How are things in Kardos? Our villages?"

"Things have improved since you left."

Wanting to believe it, Charlie recalled the ugly treatment from many Kalmar during her recent adventures out in the streets. She was grateful that Andren and Starr's guard had accompanied them. "Have you found a mate yet?"

Dorlon sighed heavy, then indicated her body and explained, "This does not lend to a mate, especially an Alpha." There wasn't any forlornness in her expression, but Charlie caught the heaviness on Dorlon's shoulders. Being a warrior and a commander had its burdens. There were thousands of soldiers and perhaps a million citizens who all relied on her leadership. The responsibilities were great and didn't lend to a romantic life. However, a Kalmar had a natural need to mate and to ignore it went against their biology.

"Perhaps there is still one for you," Charlie assured and touched her friend's knee.

Dorlon seemed unconcerned and stated, "I serve my people and that is enough."

After a grumble, Charlie quipped, "You sound like the High Commander."

"Kal honors her calling, as do I." Dorlon stared deep into Charlie and explained, "She is special and more than any Kal before her."

"Because she is a Carnec Alpha?"

Dorlon grinned a little, then nodded once. "Kalatas chose her because she is a Carnec Alpha and because she is both Omega and mostly Alpha." Kal's unique biology as a Carnec Alpha was an interesting blend of the two main breeds. Maybe it brought a balance of qualities that Kalatas needed in a ruler. Dorlon continued to school Charlie about Kal. "Kalatas is limited to what the Alpha vessel is capable of comprehending, of how the Alpha can think and what the Alpha can achieve, if anything." Dorlon's smile held pride. "As a Carnec Alpha, Kal can reach more than only Alphas."

"She can reach Omegas on a different level than simply a mate to rut into," Charlie murmured after making sense of the selection.

"And humans as well," Dorlon added.

Blinking, Charlie hadn't considered that aspect. Omegas were more tolerant and gentler by nature. They were the ones that sought peace first, but they were fierce in their own right. As a pup, Dorlon was no exception and had forged a friendship with Charlie and Raine. Andren was another example of an Omega who respected Charlie. If Kal had those Omega qualities, then she was different. "Huh," she murmured and absorbed the significant change in Kander's rulership. After a long silence, she focused on Dorlon again. "How many Omegas are in the army now?"

"About twenty percent are Omegas."

Charlie touched her brow before sweeping loose blond hair behind her ear. "That's amazing," she muttered. She remained awed by Kal, but then the dull ache returned in her chest as she realized that Kal's sacrifice was great. Charlie doubted she could ever sacrifice her identity for the good of her people. After a sigh, she eyed Dorlon and asked, "What was her name before she became Kal?" If Dorlon trained Kal, then she had to know. Would she tell Charlie or guard the secret until the end of Kal's time?

"Her old name is gone, even from me."

The answer was unexpected and left a bad taste in Charlie's mouth. She rubbed her forehead and muttered, "Until her death."

Dorlon dipped her head in agreement. "Upon her death, she will whisper her old name again." She reached for Charlie's knee, squeezing it in comfort.

Charlie breathed in Dorlon's comforting scent, which reminded her of home. She warded off the childhood memories, but a sad smile tugged at her lips. Omegas were natural assurers and protectors. Their pheromones tended to be delicate and warm, like a blanket. They could dismantle an aggressive Alpha. Charlie had missed Dorlon's unique scent.

"It's good to see you again, Dorlon." Charlie covered Dorlon's hand, holding it. At one time, she'd had a crush on Dorlon and even fought with Raine about it. Even now, the attraction was rekindled in her, but it paled to what Kal had done to her in recent days.

"You too." Dorlon ended their contact and said, "*Tah* for taking the job."

Charlie nodded once, but mentioning the job made her think more on it. "Do you know much about this Omega?"

"I have never met her," Dorlon replied, almost too fast. Her response seemed a bit scripted, but what could she be hiding from Charlie? Who was this kidnapped Omega?

Charlie squinted after the possible lie. Humming low, she considered why the kidnapped Omega had everyone on edge, especially at the initial meeting in the throne room. She was about to ask more when the office door swung open, signaling the High Commander's hasty return.

Dorlon was on her feet, concern written over her features. "What has happened, Kal?"

Charlie stood next to her friend and frowned at Kal's dark eyes and curled lip.

"The kidnappers will be here in an hour."

"*Shit*," Charlie said in English. She hurried around the sofa and approached the ruler. "They weren't due until—"

"I know," Kal cut off.

Dorlon joined the pair. "Is there anything I can do, Kal?"

After a low growl, Kal focused on Dorlon and said, "I need you to gather soldier uniforms that will fit two of the mercenaries. Gather weapons too."

"They said no soldiers," Charlie reminded.

"Fuck the terms," Kal swore. "They will accept it if they want the first run of darakar."

Despite the situation, Charlie grinned and approved of Kal's aggressive nature, not only when they were in bed. "All right. I'll get my team ready." She turned to Dorlon. "You'll bring the stuff to us?" After Dorlon's nod, she suggested, "Probably uniforms that would fit one Alpha and one Omega." She looked to Kal next. "Should we meet you on the ground floor?"

"*Ja.* I will prepare the darakar for transport."

Not waiting further, Charlie hurried out of the room, her gait getting wider with every step. She glanced over her shoulder at Andren and ordered, "Faster." She ignored Andren's dirty look, shoved the gate closed, and hit the button on the elevator. She was primed to save an Omega and collect the stills for the job.

* * *

"Yeah, we're ready to go," Charlie reported, her two crewmembers beside her along with their guards and Dorlon.

After preparing the darakar, Kal had, at some point, returned to her quarters or sent someone there. She wore her typical black overcoat that brushed the floor behind her. Its collar covered her neck and revealed the red leather on the inside, signaling her position as the High Commander. On her left side was a sword in a scabbard. It had a contoured white handle and two circular openings—a larger one between the blade and handle, then a smaller one at the pummel. The design and metal were peculiar.

Kal nodded at the mercenaries, then turned to Dorlon. Before she could give her orders, Dorlon spoke with firmness.

"I will accompany you."

Charlie raised an eyebrow and watched the silent battle of wills between former student and teacher, wondering who would win. She bit her bottom lip when Kal grumbled but moved her head in agreement. Dorlon might be the only being capable of throwing her weight around with the supreme ruler of Kander.

"The trucks are waiting for us." Kal started the march out of the Great Tower at a fast pace. Guards hurried out of her path and opened the entrance doors. On the street, several hover vehicles waited for the large group made up of Kalmar soldiers and mercenaries. Everyone followed the High Commander's orders, taking seats in the truck beds and listening to directions about the plans. Charlie was halfway into a truck with her crew when a strong hand pulled her back down to the ground.

"You are riding with me," Kal ordered her.

Charlie caught Starr's displeasure, but she offered a reassuring smile and promised, "See you there." She followed Kal to the first truck in the lineup, loading into it. Dorlon was seated on the bench to the left, so she sat down next to her, expecting Kal to sit on the opposite bench. However, Kal wedged into the remaining space on the bench, which put Charlie between the Kalmar she once had a crush on and the Kalmar who'd fucked her last night. She blushed and cursed herself.

Dorlon patted the truck's cab and signaled the driver to go. "You don't look so ridiculously human." She indicated Charlie's new attire.

Charlie glared at Dorlon, then pulled on the neckline of the black shirt under the dark jacket. "It's a little tight." She preferred jeans, a form-fitting shirt, and her leather jacket. But disguises were common in her line of work.

"You should consider losing some weight then."

Charlie growled and smacked Dorlon on the side. "I exercise plenty. It's easy to get fat in outer space." Yet she pulled on the pants at her thighs, trying to loosen them. "I don't know how you wear these so damn tight." Kal's low grunt made Charlie drop her eyes to Kal's crotch where there was an apparent bulge, and she flushed again.

Dorlon leaned in closer and whispered, "Eyes on the prize?"

Charlie snarled and withheld from hitting her again. Then she stiffened after she processed Dorlon's joke. Did her friend know what happened between her and Kal last night? Maybe Kal had told her, but Kal promised nothing would leave the bedroom. Charlie attempted to play along and said, "Shut up." Dorlon could be prodding Charlie for staring without realizing the implications. Charlie glanced at Kal, who had a neutral expression. If Kal was unconcerned, then Charlie didn't have to worry.

"The meeting point is about ten minutes from Tarrak," Kal told the pair.

"What is the plan, Kal?" Dorlon was serious again but at ease too. She and Kal seemed to hold a different comfort level between them due to their long relationship. In fact, Dorlon had known Kal longer than Charlie.

Kal leaned forward, resting her elbows on her knees so she had a view of both Charlie and Dorlon. "We will unload the darakar, then you will take command of the soldiers. They must be at least one march away from the meeting point. The mercenaries and I will handle the kidnappers when they arrive."

Charlie clenched her jaw after being referred to as a mercenary again. She expected more of Kal after their night together. *You let last night go to your head*, she chided herself. She swallowed against the burn in her throat.

"It'll only be three of you," Dorlon argued. "Is that enough?"

Kal revealed a wolfish smile.

Dorlon sighed with extra exaggeration. "Don't take unnecessary risks, Kal."

With wide eyes, Charlie sat silent and listened to the exchange. She was caught in the middle and grinned at Dorlon's ability to wrangle in Kal. Charlie needed to follow Dorlon's example and not give up ground when she stood toe-to-toe with Kal.

"*Ja*, Commander Dorlon."

After the discussion, there was no residual tension or animosity between Dorlon and Kal. They respected each other, which intrigued Charlie. With a tilt of her head, she asked, "Do these humans know Kalmarese?"

"*Ja*," Kal replied, "at least one human named Anderson."

"He's who you've been dealing with?"

Kal nodded at Charlie's question.

Frowning at the news, Charlie considered whether the human, Anderson, had a bionic port to his brain, like Raakor. There were few beings in outer space that spoke Kalmarese because the Kalmar never left the planet. However, in the past, there had been traders and linguists who had researched the language and taken it off-world.

Dorlon gazed about their location. "We're close."

Charlie fished out the techbit from its tight confines in the canvas jacket. She tapped and swiped a few times until she had their location on the map. They were near the shuttle, which Raakor would need to take to the *Pacifica* as soon as they took control of the kidnappers' spacecraft.

After a few more minutes of travel, the convoy slowed near an old, forgotten stone windmill beside a field. The seven vehicles were parked in different spots, and all at once, the soldiers hastened to unload the darakar from the one truck. It took two soldiers at a time to lift one wood crate that was filled with ingots of darakar.

Dorlon hopped out of the truck from the side, not wasting any time. Kal moved next and headed toward the tailgate but faltered when Charlie stood in her path. She raised her chin at Charlie's aggressive stance.

"Look, I get you don't have a name anymore, but I do." Charlie poked Kal in the chest and ordered, "Try using it for once." She spun around and hopped out of the truck before Kal had a chance to respond. Not that Charlie cared to wait for it. She headed to her crewmen and grinned at Starr tugging on the collar of her uniform shirt.

"You have your techbit, right?" Charlie asked Raakor first thing.

"*Ja.*" Raakor pulled the device from his pocket and confirmed that it was operating, tapping on the screen. He hadn't put on a military uniform since he couldn't pass for a Kalmar.

"I'll call after we deal with these kidnappers," Charlie explained. "You should ride with Commander Dorlon. They'll bring you back quickly enough."

Raakor nodded, then looked up from the techbit. "The shuttle is about ten clicks from here."

For one tick, Charlie had to convert the math in her head, still using old Earth measurements at times. A click was close to an Earth half mile. "Good."

Starr had her arms folded against her chest and was listening to the pair. "*Is that the same Dorlon who recommended us for the job?*" She had switched back to Jero.

"*You got it, Sherlock.*" Charlie glanced over in Dorlon's direction before she saw Starr's bewildered look and knew why. "*Sherlock Holmes was a famous detective back on Earth a long time ago.*" Sometimes it was a burden to be the solo Earthling in the crew.

Starr rolled her eyes at Charlie's human history and refocused their conversation. "*How are we handling the kidnappers when they land here?*"

"*I'm not exactly sure what the High C has in mind,*" Charlie confessed. "*But I'm sure she has a plan since she's an overbearing Alpha.*" In truth, she was relying on Kal to handle the situation.

Starr grunted.

"*What's a High C?*" Raakor asked with a furrow creasing his brow.

Starr glared at Raakor and said, "*Don't encourage—*"

"*Who doesn't know what Hi-C is?*" Charlie stared in mock disbelief at the pair. She never wasted an opportunity to tease them. "*It was the best damn sugary juice on Earth.*"

Starr moaned low and rubbed her brow before she looked over at Raakor. "*Happy now?*"

Puckering his dark lips, Raakor said, "*Human history does leave a lot to be desired.*"

Starr grinned at Raakor and chuckled.

Charlie leaned into Starr. "*Remember, you're half human.*"

"*But only half, unlike you,*" Starr fired back.

Seeing the High Commander coming toward them, Charlie bit her tongue but promised to get even with Starr. Their constant game of bantering would never end. She turned toward Kal and waited for the next details of their mission.

"We are ready, and they should be here any moment." The foldable tablet that Kal held at her side chirped at her.

Charlie retrieved her techbit and listened to Kal talking to somebody over the tablet. Connecting to the *Pacifica*'s systems, she was able to perform scans within a few leagues into outer space. "Raakor, you turned on the cloaking, right?"

"*Ja.*"

"*Ja*, Kal," a male Alpha reported from the tablet. "They radioed in that they're fifteen minutes out."

"Keep me informed of their whereabouts," Kal replied, then switched off the tablet's screen after the person confirmed the order.

"They're not far," Charlie agreed and held up the techbit's screen to Kal. "That blue circle is the *Pacifica*, and the red dot that's moving is the kidnappers' ship." She put away the techbit and said, "We should get ready. Raakor?" She looked to him and nodded at him to go.

Raakor took a backward step in Dorlon's direction and said, "Be careful." He hurried off without another word.

Charlie and Starr returned to the center, next to the crates of darakar that waited for the kidnappers. For a moment, Charlie envisioned all the crates in the cargo hold of the *Pacifica* for them to burn at their leisure or sell. Her mouth watered at the mental picture, but then Starr's low growl broke it.

Starr continued pulling on the black shirt under her jacket, then hesitated when Charlie smirked at her. "It's fucking tight."

Chuckling, Charlie watched as the solar-powered vehicles started zipping out of the field, leaving them alone. At least they wouldn't be far if the meeting unraveled. She fingered the buttstock of her rifle that was slung across her back. Its presence reassured her.

Kal joined them but was preoccupied, eyes scanning the blue sky. "They entered the planet's atmosphere."

Starr glanced at Charlie, who shrugged in response. The person who had hailed Kal earlier probably alerted Kal of the kidnappers' location.

"Kal, Kal, this is Blade Perras."

Lifting the tablet, Kal tapped the screen once and ordered, "This is Kal. Go ahead, Blade Perras."

"Scans are picking up the ship's entry into Kander's airspace. It's approximately fifty-seven marches from your location."

"Report back when it is ten marches."

"*Ja*, Kal."

Lowering the tablet, Kal continued staring upward, as if reading the skies. Charlie wondered if somehow Kal could sense the ship's movement through the planet's atmosphere, relying on the Spirit of Kalatas. "So, exactly, what is the plan when they land here?"

"I will handle them," Kal replied and never broke her concentration on the sky.

Muttering under her breath, Charlie folded her arms and decided she would let Kal handle the kidnappers alone, since Kal was being bullish again. As they stood there, she now realized that Kal had no weapon other than the old-school sword. Tightness built up in her chest. Before she could say something, another hail came over the tablet.

"Kal, Kal, this is Blade Perras again. The ship is ten marches out and beginning to slow."

Kal tapped the screen and replied, "Report if they go off course."

"*Ja*, Kal."

Lowering the tablet to her side, Kal watched the skies and remained silent for a while, then whispered, "They are here."

Scanning the blue sky, Charlie saw nothing, much less a large spaceship. She and Starr exchanged a questioning glance. But a distant woosh tickled Charlie's ear.

"Kal, Kal, this is Blade Perras. You should have a visual on the ship any tick," the soldier reported from the tablet.

Tapping the screen, Kal replied, "I have a visual." After she finished the transmission, the ship appeared in the sky, in front of them, and a distant hum was growing stronger as the vessel approached them. Kal turned to Charlie and ordered, "Stay relatively close but behind me." Without waiting for confirmation, she went to the crates and folded up the tablet until it fit in her overcoat's pocket.

Charlie and Starr followed but stayed a few paces behind the High Commander. Like Starr, Charlie retrieved the laser rifle from her back and held it in front of her. But then her damn shirt started irritating her again, so she yanked on the collar. She caught Starr's smirk and she hissed, "What?"

Starr bared her teeth in a wicked grin but lost it when the overhead noise drew her attention.

Charlie shoved a few wild strands of hair from her face when the ship's thrusters kicked up everything. She watched how the ship inched lower and lower, next to the windmill, which appeared minute in size.

"It's cargo transporter," Starr called over the wind.

"They came prepared," Charlie agreed. "It actually looks Hurr built." The images that Kal had showed her implied that the ship might be manufactured by the Hurr. If so, then Raakor would be able to hack the security in his sleep.

"We might be in luck for once."

Charlie hoped they were because they deserved it. The transporter ship's left wing clipped the windmill and knocked a few stones out of it. "What an idiot," she hollered over the thruster's roar. Her personal judgment on the pilot's skills was further solidified when the thrusters were shut off too early and the ship dropped to the ground with a boom.

Starr huffed and muttered, "Human pilots can't use stupid auto."

Rolling her eyes, Charlie decided to ignore the remark and remained focused on the task at hand. Her grip flexed against the trigger guard, ready to cut a kidnapper in half.

The ship's stern was facing them, and its large cargo bi-door split open to reveal three figures at the mouth. Two people marched down the ramp, guns at the ready and scanning for trouble, while the third person in the middle strolled down. They approached and trained their weapons on Kal first.

"I said no soldiers," the middle human snapped. His Kalmarese was choppy and slow but understandable for all of them. When he turned his head, the bionic port on his neck, next to his jaw, confirmed Charlie's earlier suspicions that he had tech integrated into his brain. It's possible the other humans had the same and had downloaded Kalmarese.

"You are Anderson," Kal stated.

Anderson, the middle human, narrowed his eyes, then declared, "I want them to toss their weapons or"—he signaled the person to his left—"Jett will end your reign."

Upon hearing the threat, Charlie aimed the rifle toward the kidnappers and was tempted to put a hole in them until Kal looked at her. She grumbled and glowered at the kidnappers.

"Lower your weapons," Kal ordered. But when Charlie hesitated, she growled. "Now."

Grinding her teeth, Charlie loosened her grip and remembered to play along a little. "*Ja*, Kal." She glanced at Starr, who copied her, but their attention remained on the kidnappers in front of Kal.

"Maya, keep an eye on those thickheaded Kalmar and make sure there're no heroics," Anderson ordered in Kalamarese and waited until Maya was closer to Charlie and Starr with a rifle trained on them. He then smiled at Kal. "And you are the High Commander of Kander." He held out his hands and taunted, "Such a lovely planet, and might I add, one that's full of resources."

Kal remained silent, hands loosely at her side. However, Charlie sensed the dark presence in Kal building up as Anderson mocked both Kal and her planet. In that instant, she wondered if the mounting energy around Kal was the Spirit of Kalatas. She couldn't ignore the crawl of her skin or the way the air crackled with power.

"Including darakar," Anderson stated, with excitement. "Lots of darakar."

Kal took a side step and held out her arm toward the stack of ten crates that held the fuel. "The first load as requested for the Omega."

Anderson clapped his hands together and beamed further upon seeing the partial ransom. "How long will it take to prepare the second load?"

"Nine rotations of our planet," Kal replied.

Anderson tilted his head and stared at the crates before nodding a few times. "I've further considered the terms of our agreement." His sickening smile made Charlie want to wring his neck. "Rather than ten loads, we will take twenty for the Omega's release."

"Twenty?" Kal echoed in disdain and rising anger.

Jett laughed at the High Commander's reaction and joked, "I told you to make it thirty, boss."

Anderson waved him off and argued, "We're not greedy." After giving Jett a pointed look, he smiled at Kal but it melted away. "Think of us as reasonable."

What an asshole, Charlie concluded. She could imagine Kal's expression, but she felt every tendril of godhood pulsing off Kal. Her heart jumped into overdrive while she prepared for a fight. Everything went to absolute hell in half a heartbeat, and she worked on instincts.

Kal had unsheathed her sword, which had been ignored by the kidnappers as a threat. She slashed through Jett's wrists, cutting off his hands from the rifle. She spun around with the blade and drove the tip into Anderson's gut.

Maya had stumbled away but not before firing shots at the High Commander. Growling low, Kal moved the sword so fast it was a blur, and the laser shots bounced off the flat of the blade. She stalked closer to Maya, who continued firing at her, but repelled every shot.

Before it was too late, Charlie scooped up the laser rifle and fired at Maya, knocking her back on the ground.

Kal turned around and threw the sword into Jett's chest, ending his maddening screams.

Charlie hurried over to Anderson and felt Starr on her heels. She pointed the gun at him and watched him clutch his stomach, his hands covered in blood.

After ripping the sword from Jett, Kal stalked over to Anderson and flipped the handle in her grip so the tip pointed downward. Lifting the sword above her head, she growled and declared, "The Omega is worth more than all of the planet's darakar."

"Wait!" Anderson yelled, one hand up. "I can—" His words were cut off by the white blade that sliced through his open mouth and pierced his brain.

For good measure, Kal wrenched the blade hard, then pulled it free from the corpse. She proceeded to wipe the blood onto Anderson's clothes.

Charlie blew out a breath and looked at the three dead kidnappers. "Well, that was really—"

"Unexpected," Starr supplied.

"*Joh*." Charlie shook her head and argued, "I mean it was, but it was really badass." She heard Kal's low but thick rumble, and she wondered if Starr caught it. She grabbed the techbit from her jacket and radioed Raakor to come back.

Kal sheathed the sword and appeared calm after the fight. She approached the ship's open bay.

Charlie followed, with Starr at her side, both of them looking over the ship's exterior details. All the characteristics indicated that the ship was built by a Hurr company, a rather well-known one in the galaxy.

Standing at the bottom of the ramp, Kal peered into the dimly lit mouth but never boarded it.

Starr entered the vessel, rifle at the ready and searching for any surprises.

"It's definitely a transporter," Charlie mentioned once she came to Kal near the metal beast. After a quiet moment, she tilted her head and asked, "Have you been in space yet?"

"*Joh.*"

Frowning, Charlie suspected Kal had little to no desire to ride into outer space unless necessary. She cleared her throat and said, "You were amazing with that sword." Earlier, she had noticed the blade was forged from a white metal that had a reflective glass-like surface. "What is it made from?"

"A rare alloy called *viton.* It is a precise combination of *villion* and *diton* metals that are forged using darakar." Kal rested her hand on the hilt, gripping it. "It is the Sword of Kalatas."

Curious about the blade's history, Charlie folded her arms, then turned to Kal. "How did you know it would stop the lectra blasts?"

Kal flashed a toothy smile and leaned closer to Charlie. "I was not certain." Upon hearing the convoy's return, she joined them and barked out orders to have the darakar reloaded into the trucks.

Raakor rushed to Charlie and carried a heavy satchel filled with their gear. "It's a Hurrion Grey 231B Transporter," he stated while looking over the ship.

Charlie smirked, relieved they were catching a break. "Come on." Together they hurried through the metal hallways and went to the cockpit where Starr was seated in the copilot's spot.

Raakor jumped into the pilot's seat with his special tech. "It'll probably take me ten ticks unless…"

"Unless what?" Charlie narrowed her eyes at Raakor's frustrated look. "What?"

"It has a biometric scan requirement before I can even power anything."

"Can you bypass it?" Starr asked.

"*Ja*, but that'll waste more time." Raakor looked at them and said, "It requires a scan of his palm."

Starr grunted, popped up from the chair, and marched off with Charlie on her heels. Outside, the Kalmar soldiers were carrying away the last crate and starting to collect the dead bodies. Starr went to Anderson's body and told the two soldiers to back off.

Charlie halted when the two soldiers bared their teeth at Starr, but Kal ordered them to stand down. "We need his hand for a biometric scan," she explained.

Starr had her arms hooked under Anderson's body and started to drag him. But she stiffened when Kal approached with the sword out.

With a single clean cut, Anderson's hand was removed, picked up, and tossed over to Charlie in less than five ticks. But Charlie fumbled with the hand and let it drop to the ground, squealing in reaction. "*Vuk*," she hissed and turned her glare from the offending hand to Kal. "I hate decapitated body parts."

With a smirk, Starr came over and snatched the hand from the ground, then held it up in front of Charlie, not at all bothered by it. "Only head is decapitated. It a severed hand."

"Shut up," Charlie said and grumbled. Yet Starr's banter was a sign that the flare-up was gone or nearly gone, and that gave Charlie some relief.

Starr chuckled on her way past Charlie and muttered, "I like her style, for an Alpha."

After rolling her eyes, Charlie followed and decided to get changed from the overly tight clothes into her regular attire. Starr also retrieved her clothes from Raakor's duffel bag.

"It's done," Raakor announced and stepped out of the cockpit. "I set up a link to the *Pacifica*, so we can communicate."

Charlie shrugged on her leather jacket. "Perfect."

"But there's one problem," Raakor mentioned and hesitated when Charlie gave him a menacing look. "It's an ancient Hurr design and requires three operators; one to fly, one to navigate, and one to land."

Starr smacked the bulkhead next to her and swore. She huffed and walked away from the pair, but turned when Charlie spoke again.

"I thought this thing had auto."

Raakor shook his head at Charlie and explained, "It's a 231B. It's older than this planet."

"We need Raakor to lead us with the *Pacifica*," Starr reminded them.

Humming low and staring at the floor, Charlie weighed the options and asked, "Sturdy boat, right?" She raised an eyebrow at Raakor. As long as it was safe, then she could make it work.

"The 231Bs are still used for a reason," Raakor argued.

"I got an idea then," Charlie declared and started to the stern again.

"Have," Starr corrected.

"I like you better when you're flaring." Charlie ordered her team to wait at the mouth of the ship while she handled the situation. She marched over to the High Commander, who was waiting for her while the soldiers loaded into the trucks.

"Can you fly the ship?" Kal asked.

"*Ja*, but there's a problem." Charlie paused, folded her arms, and went in for the kill. "I need a volunteer." She gestured at the transporter vessel and said, "It was designed to fly with three heads. Raakor needs to return to our ship so he can follow us, or else the escape plan might get really messy."

Kal clenched her jaw and studied the ship before vehemently declaring, "This was not a part of the agreement. I will not risk another one of my people's lives."

Taking a deep breath, Charlie did her best to remain calm rather than rise to Kal's aggressive nature. "And this time the risk is worth it."

Kal shifted closer into Charlie's space and growled, "I hired you to—"

"Screw the job! I am asking you to trust me," Charlie declared in a heated voice, losing her control. "You trusted me last night," she whispered. "Trust me with this." Even as she felt Kal's raw power building up, she didn't surrender to it, and swore, "I will bring both your people back to you."

After a low huff, Kal pivoted and yelled, "Andren!"

Charlie released a strangled breath and allowed the tension to recede from her chest. She thanked the Celestial Fates or whoever it was that gave Kal a measure of clarity.

"*Ja*, Kal?" Andren asked once she approached them. She was carrying a laser rifle between her hands, toying with it a little.

"The mercenaries require assistance flying the kidnappers' ship." Kal hesitated, then asked, "Are you willing to help them? You may refuse, and it will not be a mark against your honor."

Andren studied the ship behind Charlie for a moment, then said, "I wouldn't know how to fly it."

"You don't have to fly it. We'll take care of that. You simply have to help us land it. It's not hard, and we can show you what to do." A stolen glance at Kal told Charlie that they both were anxious about Andren's decision.

Finally, Andren nodded and had a confident air to her.

Charlie remained calm but celebrated on the inside, almost wanting to kiss Andren. "*Tah,*" she offered and gave a sincere smile. Without Andren, they would have to scrap the current plan after Kal's hard work to organize it. "Starr will show you thc ship."

Andren slung the rifle onto her back, then boarded the vessel.

"And *tah* for trusting me," Charlie whispered to Kal.

"It is not a matter of trust," Kal said, and a shadow passed over her features. "I can no longer protect my people once they are off-world."

Charlie sighed and whispered, "But I will." Then she sensed Raakor coming up to them, so she turned to him. "We're going to brief Andren on the landing systems. We should be ready by the time you get to the *Pacifica*."

Raakor nodded and said, "See you in space, boss." He then tossed the severed body part at Charlie. "*Tah* for the hand too," he said, then left for the vehicles to get a ride to the shuttle.

After a yelp, Charlie dropped the offending body part and warily eyed it on the ground, even when Kal picked it up. She cleared her throat in hopes her voice wasn't a squeak. "I should go." But she remained there because Kal's expression held her in place. For the first time, there were hints of true concern on her face and a deeper concern in those green eyes. Kal's care tightened around Charlie's heart, and she wanted to touch Kal.

"Bring both Omegas back to me," Kal said with half authority and half plea. "And be careful out there."

Charlie nodded once and turned to go, yet faltered again, surprised by Kal's last words.

"*Krafka*, Charlie."

Gazing over her shoulder, Charlie was weak after hearing Kal's soft but sincere use of her name. She swallowed hard and hoped her voice came out more confident compared to her thundering heart. The job had become personal. "I promise, Kal."

Chapter 8

"Bay doors are closed and sealed," Andren called out.

Reaching overhead in the cockpit, Charlie flipped switches but continued watching the flickering onboard dual screens that fed data about the transporter's systems. "Prepare to ignite engines," she yelled through the cockpit.

Starr was swiping her finger across the single large screen in front of her. "Clear!"

Charlie pushed the twin buttons together, listening to the engines firing to life without any hesitation, but the roar overwhelmed the cockpit. "Holy fuck!"

Starr covered her own ears, then held up a headset and yanked them on over her head. She twisted in the seat and yelled at Andren to put hers on.

After adjusting the wireless headset, Charlie asked, "How in the hell does this ship not have noise dampening on it?"

"It's that old," Starr argued.

"Andren, can you hear us?" Charlie checked and peered over her shoulder to the third seat behind her and Starr.

"*Ja.* I can hear you both," Andren reported.

"No auto, no noise dampening, and now headsets. What's next?" Charlie muttered over the headset's comms, but her focus was on the panels all around her. She was used to flying ships that were streamlined and simpler than this transporter, and it took her a few extra ticks to understand everything.

"I have the route the kidnappers took to get here," Starr reported.

Charlie perked up at the news. "Where we headed, navigator?" She grinned when Starr gave her a death glare, but then Starr had a worried look when she looked back at the navigation screen. "Where, Starr?"

"Nowhere."

After a groan, Charlie's head thudded against the chair, and she rubbed her forehead.

"Nowhere?" Andren asked, confusion lacing her tone.

"It's a wasteland," Charlie explained. "It's a planet that used to be called Golden Ring before the entire place got wiped out."

"What happened to it?"

Charlie frowned at Andren's curiosity about the dead planet. "It was destroyed by the Sworne." She sat up after noticing the engines were ready for takeoff. "Engines are warm."

"Quickest route to Nowhere has been mapped," Starr reported. "Andren, do you remember what to do?"

"*Ja.*"

"Time to take off then," Charlie announced and pushed the twin throttles to increase the engine's thrust. She already felt the ship lifting off the ground, but she had trouble balancing it due to the landing gears being extended and magnetized to the ground. "Andren, I need you to shut off the anchoring system, or we're going to slam back down." She growled from the force against the control stick between her hands. "Like, right fucking now!"

Starr had her hands on the buckles of her chair, ignoring the risks of moving around when the ship was flying.

"Got it," Andren declared.

The resistance vanished, and the engines launched the ship into the air without any control. The right wing slammed into the old windmill, shearing off the top of it.

"Shit, shit, shit." Charlie's mantra continued as she fought with the stick and played with the throttle until the vessel and engines became equal forces again, allowing things to hover high above the ground. "Timing. We have to work on that." After checking a few systems, she increased the throttle and steered the ship toward the heavens. "And here we go!"

Starr gripped the chair's arms, knuckles going white. After a few ticks, she opened her eyes and said, "I'll radio Raakor." She tapped the panel and went to work.

"How are you doing, Andren?" Charlie asked over the comms and received a pained whimper in response, which made her chuckle. "It'll get easier," she lied. She glanced at Starr, who was talking to Raakor over the radios. It was a perfect opportunity to spice up the flight back to outer space, so she commanded, "Nova, play my MJ list, starting with 'Smooth Criminal.'"

"MJ list now playing," the techbit announced, and Michael Jackson's voice filled the ship's internal comms system. Happy to have music again, Charlie sang with Michael Jackson while she flew the transporter through Kander's atmosphere, breaking through a developing storm front that jostled the ship.

"You're kidding me," Starr complained when she switched back to the ship's internal comms. Her voice caused the comms to fade Michael Jackson's voice to the background.

Charlie chose to ignore the remark about the music and asked, "Where's Raakor?"

"He load into the *Pacifica*."

"Perfect." Charlie smiled. Their plans were playing out well so far. Maybe Lady Luck was on their side again.

"We're about two marches from breaking Kander's gravity." Starr continued using the touch panel and then gave a low sigh.

"Now what?"

Starr looked over at Charlie. "There's no gravity system on the ship."

"That's a funny one, Starr."

"It's not a joke."

A long silence ensued until Andren's weakened voice interrupted Michael Jackson's singing. "What does that mean?"

"It means tighten your belts," Charlie replied.

Starr chuckled while rubbing her forehead and offered, "At least we have sufficient heat on this ancient bathtub."

A sudden yelp from Andren made Charlie glance back at her and grin. Like the others, she felt the weightlessness begin to lift her from the seat. She recalled the first time she'd been weightless in outer space when she was a kid, feeling like Superman. Nothing compared to it, not even being underwater, and Charlie still loved the sensation.

However, Starr always had a different opinion about it as she clutched her stomach. Andren was doing the same, both of their natural Kalmar genetics refusing to accept the off-world experience. It was almost as if Kalatas was willing its people to remain on the planet.

Starr pressed the headset against her right ear, tapping on the screen. "You're on the comms now, Raakor."

"The *Pacifica* is ready to fly," Raakor reported over the radio. "I have a visual on you."

"And I have a visual on you," Charlie replied. "The kidnappers came from Nowhere."

"*Ja*, that's what Starr said. Do we have a course plotted?"

Starr was moving her hands fast on the screen. "I'm sharing the course with you now, Raakor." She shook her head and mentioned, "It's going to take at least two hours to get to Nowhere, provided a solar storm doesn't slow us down."

"It's a boring flight to Nowhere," Raakor agreed. "The final reaches of the galaxy."

Charlie watched a heads-up hologram flicker and solidify with a basic map route to Nowhere, including a moving dot that was their ship. The transporter had an ancient navigation system that required Starr to perform dead reckoning, looking outside the cockpit for what was around them that matched up to the charts' markers to reconcile their location in outer space. Dead reckoning had been an easy navigation method before light speed engines were born and required more sophisticated systems. Thankfully, they had the *Pacifica* ahead of them for more advanced navigation.

"Is that another ship?" Andren asked over the comms.

Nibbling on her lip, Charlie stared out the front windows and watched as they approached the ghost ship drifting outside Kander's orbit. As they came closer, the details of the enormous black starship became noticeable. It had long ago been abandoned and since then looted and stripped by pirates, mercenaries, and traders. For once, Charlie felt a little nausea at seeing the starship after so long, but she re-boxed her emotions and returned them to the past where they belonged.

"It's the *Liberator*," Andren concluded.

"It was," Charlie murmured over the comms before shifting in the seat. "We're clear of the solar system, and the ships are linked. Following your lead, Raakor." She reached for a switch, fingering it warily because she knew the powerful engines were recently bolted onto the ship that once had much slower, decaying engines on it. If the kidnappers made the journey here, then maybe they would survive too. She took a deep breath and whispered, "Let's hope this works right."

"Going to light speed in four, three, two—" Raakor counted down over the comms.

"One," Charlie declared with Raakor and pushed the button that surged the engines to full power.

* * *

"We're coming up on fifteen leagues from the dorsum side of the Golden solar system," Raakor informed everyone over the comms.

"We'll drop from light speed at ten leagues. I don't want to get in the range of any detection systems that these kidnappers might have," Charlie said. In the distance, the solar system's single yellow sun glowed, welcoming them even though the Sworne having once been there and marred the solar system. "It should be close enough for you to perform scans of Golden Ring."

Starr was shaking her head. "I don't know what these kidnappers were thinking." She looked over at Charlie. "Making a base of operations on Golden Ring is stupid."

"Everything has to be brought in," Raakor agreed.

"Is there anything left of the planet?" Andren asked them.

"*Joh*," Charlie replied. "It's a decimated and broken rock, literally."

"And its people?"

"All dead. Completely wiped out by the Sworne," Charlie replied. She focused on the flight when they neared the solar system. "They took out Golden Ring before they came to Earth."

Together, the ships receded from light speed, and everyone took in the view of the Golden solar system. It was made up of one star, five planets, and an outer asteroid belt on a forty-five degree tilt from the planets' plane. Golden Ring was the fourth planet, distinguishable by its two broken halves orbiting the sun. Around the fragmented planet were trillions of ice and rock particles scattered about like shattered glass, at one time having formed the beautiful golden rings of the planet before its destruction.

"What are your scans pulling up, Raakor?" Charlie asked.

"Sending them over now."

In a few ticks, Charlie had full imagery of Golden Ring's bleak, rocky surface. "So it looks like they've set up a temporary camp. What's the white beam in the center, Raakor?"

"I believe it's an oxygenator," Raakor replied. "It creates a dome around the camp and produces air for them. Oxygen levels on Golden Ring are probably ten percent to nil by now."

"More like hazardous," Starr argued.

For a moment, Charlie stared at the images of the camp, but then she zoomed in and studied a building more. Her crew remained quiet, letting her work through the scenarios for their plan of attack. The building wasn't large and acted as a homebase for the kidnappers. There was probably a mess hall, a few quarters, an office or two, and storage areas. It wouldn't take them long to sweep the building.

"What weapons do we have?"

Starr looked over at Charlie and went down the list of what she inventoried in the duffel bag. "Four rifles, six handguns, ten photon grenades, a dagger." She pointed over her shoulder at Andren, who carried a blade. "And your Grasshopper."

Charlie beamed and joked, "You're so good to me, Raakor." She loved her Grasshopper and found it handy even though opponents laughed at her when she pointed it at them. Depending on the setting, the tiny gun had one to three shots before it discharged. But the shots held a punch.

Starr rolled her eyes and shifted in the seat. "What's the plan then?"

Charlie straightened and went over how they were going to handle the kidnappers. From her best guess, there were anywhere from two to twenty kidnappers down in the camp. Some could be away from the homebase, off on missions. They needed to capture one good squealer so they could locate the Omega. All the while, Raakor would wait in the shadows with their escape route in case it became ugly. In truth, Charlie was less concerned about capturing any kidnappers now that the valuable darakar was promised to her, except maybe for the leader.

"All right, are we clear?" Charlie checked with her team, including Andren. After everyone agreed, she increased the transporter's throttle and aimed for Golden Ring. In a few ticks, they were only leagues away from the planet, so she slowed down again.

"Transmission link coming in," Starr reported.

"Keep the video off, and turn down the ship's radio power to distort the audio."

Starr made the adjustments, then warned, "Transmitting now."

"Anderssson, what in Farsssa's titsss took you so long?"

Charlie's eyebrows hiked up at hearing a Gyr's distinct voice, and she exchanged a glance with Starr. She cleared her throat and switched to using Jero. "*Anderson is busy in the head.*"

"Maya?" the Gyr hissed. "*I didn't think you flew.*"

Rolling her eyes, Charlie huffed at the Gyr's voice. It reminded her of a leaking car tire. "*I can fly enough.*" She started prepping the transporter for entry into Golden Ring's meager atmosphere. "*We're a league from the planet coming in to land.*"

"*How far?*" the Gyr demanded. "*You're breaking up.*"

"*A league from the damn planet,*" Charlie replied louder but knew Starr had lowered the radio's power so that the Gyr didn't have a chance to figure out that Charlie wasn't Maya. An interrupted transmission was a perfect way to end it sooner.

"*Fine! And tell Anderssson to be careful landing with the darakar.*"

"*Roger that.*" Charlie cringed at her mistake of using Earth lingo, but she cut the conversation short. "*Maya out.*" She gave Starr a pointed look.

"Transmission ended," Starr assured in Kalmarese.

"You think he heard?" Charlie asked, hoping the Gyr missed her aviation slang.

Starr shrugged and then grinned over at Charlie. "You are only human."

"Shut up," Charlie fired back and grumbled when Andren's chuckle came over the comms. "Time to get serious." Ahead of them, the larger half of the planet came into view as the transporter flew underneath its broken rings. "Andren, do you remember what Starr showed you to do for the landing system?"

"*Ja.* It's three steps: levers first, make sure the lights go green, and then engage the anchoring system when you call it."

"Exactly," Charlie agreed. "And if you switch on that anchoring system too soon, we could crash."

"*Ja.*"

Charlie could tell that they were clear. Even if they did bang up the old boat, she didn't care since it wasn't hers. "How are we looking, Starr?"

"Keep a magnetic heading of 1-8-5. You should see the camp any tick now."

Charlie scanned all the instruments, ensuring she retained full control. A slight jolt to the ship told her they'd entered the planet's weak atmosphere, and her butt sank back into the seat.

"Gravity," Starr reported.

"I see the oxygenator's beam." Charlie had a visual on the camp's location on the half planet. "Hold tight. Might get bumpy from here." She tightened her grip on the controls.

Andren growled low when the vessel jerked up and down from turbulence.

Pulling back on the throttle, Charlie slowed the ship's descent and prepared to make a perfect landing with the old boat. But she was missing one key ingredient to the landing, and so she ordered, "Nova, play the Oldies list on shuffle. Begin with 'Dancing in the Dark.'"

"Playing Oldies list," the techbit announced over the comms. Starr was too preoccupied tearing her nails into the copilot's seat to comment on Charlie's human music.

Soon the base came into full view as the transporter leveled off high above the ground. Charlie located the landing site at the kidnapper's base and eased the throttle back to a few pulses above idle. She pulled the headset's mic away from her mouth and sang the lyrics alongside Bruce Springsteen.

With the landing pad below, Charlie put both hands on the stick and maneuvered the ship down. As the digital altimeter gave readings, she readied to give Andren the signal. "Prepare the landing gears."

"*Ja.*" After a moment, Andren reported, "Gears are down and locked."

"Put your hand on the anchoring switch," Charlie advised and continued guiding the ship closer to the ground. "Anchors away." The anchoring system became active, creating a magnetic pull toward the planet. Charlie kept a firm grip on the stick, landing the ship with perfect skill.

Once landed, Charlie and Starr hastened to shut down the ship's engines and systems, knowing they had little time to get ready. A quick check on Andren confirmed she had pale features from the flight.

While Starr dug out the weapons, Charlie knelt in front of Andren and reached into her leather jacket. "Take deep breaths," she advised. "Get more oxygen in your blood, and it'll pass quicker."

Andren did as she was instructed and held on to the chair.

Charlie ejected an earpiece from the techbit and inserted it into her left ear. "Nova, connect with the *Pacifica*." While she waited, she focused on Andren again. "Any better?"

After a nod, Andren unbuckled the harness and lap belt.

"Connection established," the techbit announced in the earpiece.

"Raakor, do you read me?"

"I read you," Raakor replied over the secure comms.

"We landed and are about to start Operation Trojan Horse."

Andren stood up to test her weak legs, and Charlie had to catch her. She growled low and huffed before she lifted off Charlie.

"It's your first time flying," Charlie reminded.

Andren took more steps, finding her strength again. She picked up her laser rifle from the bench seat where she'd left it earlier, then joined Starr and Charlie.

"Do you hear me, Raakor?" Starr asked through the comms.

"I read you," Raakor replied.

Charlie moved fast, snatching weapons from the duffel, and offering a lectra handgun to Andren. "You'll need this." Once Andren took it, she explained, "It's like a laser handgun, but you can control the power." She indicated the switch that had three placements. "The second or third place will kill the person; the first one will stun."

Andren nodded and tucked the handgun into her waistband, hidden from sight.

The most important weapon was Charlie's Grasshopper, which conformed to the palm of her hand. She attached it to the front of her utility belt, hidden by her jacket. Next, she slung a lectra rifle across her back while Starr took two of them. She offered the last one to Andren, who declined the weapon. Charlie shrugged and put the last rifle on her back with the other one. She then grabbed the laser rifle that came from Kander.

"You're using that old thing?"

"Don't get judgy," Charlie argued. "There's nothing wrong with a good, straight-shooting, old-school laser rifle." She carried the rifle with both hands and said, "Let's lure the suckers in and start this party."

Starr signaled for Andren to follow her to the stern, closer to the cargo bay.

"Opening bay doors," Charlie announced over the comms after reaching above Andren's former seat. She switched on only one row of lights in the cargo bay, right down the center. It would be enough to illuminate anybody entering the ship, but still hid her and the team. Hurrying through the ship, she joined the team near the cargo bay and cursed Starr for her usual arrogance.

Starr had taken position directly in the center of the empty bay but flat on her stomach with both rifles ready to fire.

Charlie and Andren hid behind a set of bulkheads used for shielding against the enemies.

"You don't have to do this," Charlie told Andren, who had done plenty for them. Kal had asked Charlie to bring back both Omegas. But it was more than an arrangement, Charlie admired Andren and wanted to ensure her safety.

Andren revealed a dark, toothy smile that showed off her canines. "I'm already in this."

Charlie sighed and muttered, "The High Commander will kill me if something happens to you."

"*Tah* for your touching concern."

Charlie glared over at Andren, hearing the sarcasm in her tone. "I do care, actually." She dropped her shoulders when Andren's smirk crumbled under Charlie's honesty.

"I know." Andren toyed with the rifle's trigger and glanced past the bulkhead. "That's why Omegas and Betas get along so well."

With a furrowed brow, Charlie noticed the slur name for humans on Kander was said with respect rather than contempt. Had the Kalmar and humans on Kander made strides? She wanted to know more, but a man's yell had her peering past the bulkhead.

"Anderson!" a male human yelled and continued to climb the ramp into the transporter. "Jett?"

Other footsteps followed the man, but Charlie had a hard time telling how many people were entering or surrounding the vessel. She bit her lip and waited for Starr to make the first move.

"*Where the fuck is the darakar?*" he demanded in Jero and was answered by an onslaught of laser shots.

Pure hell broke out inside the cargo bay as laser shots flew in every direction, most striking the kidnappers at the bay's open mouth. All the screams and yells rallied a small band of kidnappers from the base, their gunfire overwhelming Charlie's crew.

"Charlie!" Starr hollered over the din.

Charlie snatched a proton grenade, popped the pin, and chucked it across the bay. The grenade hit the top of the ramp, then rolled down to the handful of kidnappers, who missed its arrival. Ducking behind the bulkhead, Charlie closed her eyes and braced for the explosion that ripped across the entrance of the transporter's bay. She hoped Starr was unharmed.

Once the explosion burned off, everything became dark again, and Charlie was able to see Starr still on the floor of the bay. "Damn it," she hissed and ran over to Starr, falling to her knees. "Starr? Starr?" She pushed on Starr's shoulder and urged, "Come on, Starr." A throaty laugh rang in Charlie's ears. She sighed in relief.

Starr rolled onto her back and grinned. "I love grenades." She blinked a few times, then sat up.

"We've got to move," Charlie ordered and peered up when Andren joined them.

"I think we have lot heads collect later," Starr joked when she climbed to her feet. She slung one rifle over her back, then carried the second one with both hands.

"Let's go." Charlie danced through body parts toward the ramp and pressed her back against the entrance's frame, scanning for trouble around the base. The drumming of her heart grew louder the closer she was to their next fight.

Andren came to her side and sniffed the air. "I only smell humans."

"Well, we know there's at least one Gyr." Charlie looked across to Starr and said, "We're going through that entrance." She pointed at the metal door straight ahead that was several hundred paces from them. "Can you break it down?" She hated to waste grenades.

"I think so."

"We'll cover your six," Charlie promised. "We have to stay close together, Andren." She received a curt nod from Andren.

Starr edged out first and looked around the open grounds. "There has to be at least ten dead out here."

Charlie rushed down the ramp with Andren at her side. Together, they watched Starr's back as they made their way to the door of the metal building. "Raakor, it would be a good time to load into the shuttle."

"*Ja*, boss," Raakor replied over the comms. "Have we decided how we're transporting five people in a four-place shuttle?"

Charlie rolled her eyes and sighed. "Somebody is sitting in someone's lap. Just get down here." She peered over her shoulder when Starr began kicking the door, which buckled under her strength. After Starr had the entrance opened for them, they moved into a narrow hallway and scanned the immediate area for trouble.

Charlie squeezed past and went first, taking the lead. "Andren, stay behind me. Starr, watch our backs." As a single unit, they traveled down the hallway and looked for any clues to the whereabouts of the kidnapped Omega.

"There can no be many left," Starr whispered in choppy Kalmarese.

After an agreeing nod, Charlie continued through the building and arrived at a T with no indications what was in either direction. She cursed low and looked over at Starr. "Left or right?"

Before Starr could reply, a laser shot flew down from the left hallway, grazing past Charlie's shoulder. Charlie yelped and cussed in English before stumbling a step. The blast missed her, but it stole her breath.

Andren reacted first and fired the lectra handgun, hitting the kidnapper in the chest.

Charlie gawked at Andren's quick reaction and was grateful. "Nice job." She grinned at Andren, then ran down the hallway to the collapsed female human. Andren and Starr followed on her heels.

Andren sniffed the air and whispered, "She reeks of fear."

"Hmmm." Charlie hoped it would work to their benefit as she studied the paralyzed kidnapper. She knelt with the rifle's barrel pressed into the woman's chest. "*Let's start with your name,*" she said in Jero.

The kidnapper remained silent until Charlie slid the barrel to her neck.

"*Name,*" Charlie ordered and placed her finger over the trigger.

"Dakota." The kidnapper, Dakota, moved a few fingers as the paralysis started to fade. Her breaths were less labored.

"*Where's the kidnapped Omega?*" Charlie asked.

"*Screw you!*" Dakota bared her teeth. "*Go ahead and shoot me.*" The flintiness of her gaze didn't affect Charlie in any manner.

Tilting her head, Charlie frowned and realized she needed to motivate Dakota to talk to them. "*We really don't have a lot of time to waste,*" she explained. "*So my friend here*"—she indicated Andren—"*is a Kalmar who's very unhappy that you took one of her people.*"

Dakota's eyes darted between Charlie and Andren. Her breaths became labored.

"*She's also very good with a dagger.*" Charlie peered up at Andren and switched to Kalmarese. "Use your dagger on our new friend."

Andren unsheathed the blade, which was both long and wide with a slight curve to it. She used the tip to lift Dakota's shirt, exposing skin. She grazed the tip forward and drew a line of blood.

"*Now you can tell us what we need to know or...*" Charlie peered up at Andren, switched tongues, and asked, "Should we start with fingers first?" She smirked when Andren nodded once, then looked down at Dakota again. "*Which hand do you dislike more?*"

Dakota scrambled backward on her hands and feet. The paralyzing effects were gone or close to it. "*N-n-no.*"

Andren growled while stepping forward and raised the blade overhead.

"*Sh-sh-she's being held down this hallway, then to the left, and on the second right,*" Dakota confessed and raised a hand. "*In a room with the number 11.*"

"*Excellent.*" Charlie chuckled at her win, grateful for their hostage's weak loyalty. She snared Dakota by her shirt and hauled her up, then shoved her backward toward Andren. "*You're coming with us. I'm not great at remembering directions.*"

Andren hooked a hand around her new hostage's shoulder and pressed the blade against the side of her neck. She forced Dakota forward, taking the lead in the hallway.

"Charlie," Raakor called over the comms, "I entered the atmosphere or what's left of it."

"Roger that," Charlie replied. "I need you to stay a few marches away from the base until we get this Omega."

"Understood."

Andren kept a firm hand on Dakota's shoulder and nudged her forward.

"Nothing like cold, sharp metal to inspire somebody," Charlie muttered. Behind them, Starr was covering their backs.

At the end of the hall, they turned to the left, then the second right brought them to a shorter hallway that ended with three different doors, each with a number. Andren shoved Dakota to door fifty-one and ordered, "Open it."

"*Unlock the door,*" Charlie translated.

Dakota narrowed her eyes at the mercenaries from over her shoulder but approached the biometric pad. She raised her hand to it, allowing the system to scan her.

"*At least we don't have to sever her hand like we did with Anderson,*" Starr joked and chuckled at the wary glance from Dakota.

Charlie smirked at Dakota's paled features after the mention of Anderson. "*Open the door,*" she commanded when the latching system released.

After a moment of hesitation, Dakota tapped the access button, and the door slid to the left. She was shoved into the room, but caught herself from hitting the floor.

Charlie and Starr fanned out on either side of Andren, rifles at the ready.

"*That'sss far enough,*" a Gyr ordered in the Jero tongue.

Several paces in front of them was the Gyr, with an arm across a female hostage's chest and a gun pressed to her temple. The hostage had a black bag over her head, but Charlie still heard her occasional whimper. When Andren took a step closer, Charlie surmised it was the kidnapped Omega.

"*Not another move,*" the Gyr snapped.

"Stay still," Charlie translated to Andren. "It'll be fine." She shifted her attention to Dakota and teased, "*Traitor.*"

"*Take their weaponsss, Dakota.*"

Andren's hostage, Dakota, turned on her heels and revealed her smug look, now that she had the upper hand. "*You didn't really think it was that easy?*"

Charlie sighed, still believing it was easy, because it seemed Dakota and the Gyr were the last ones. There were no other kidnappers coming to assist them, and Charlie liked the odds as her quick mind formulated a plan.

Dakota started with Andren and ordered, "*Toss your blade.*"

Regardless of the language barrier, Andren caught on and lifted the blade's tip near Dakota's face, then dropped it to the floor.

Dakota kicked it aside, then ordered, "*Everything. Now.*"

Everyone stripped their weapons from their bodies, creating a chorus of metal striking the stone floor. A tense silence followed. Dakota grabbed one of the lectra handguns for herself.

"*Ssso, the High Commander sssent one of her own, a human, and a Kalman mix,*" the Gyr declared. "*What a pathetic team.*"

Charlie snorted but hid it by covering her nose. She cleared her throat and pretended to be concerned about the current situation. Dakota neared the Gyr, which gave Charlie a better view of him under the bleak overhead lights.

Starr growled and took a step forward with her hands fisted at her side.

"*Ssstop,*" the Gyr hissed and dug the gun into the Omega's head.

Charlie narrowed her eyes, then her memory placed the Gyr's familiar features. "*You were on Lerto.*" She cursed under her breath, hoping he forgot about Raakor.

"Barr," the Gyr supplied.

Needing a distraction, Charlie fixed a smile and said, "*Listen, Barr, we'll cut you and Dakota a deal.*" She shrugged and offered, "*If you give us the Omega and let us go, then we won't take you back to Kander with us. You can just go on your way.*" She looked over at Starr, who gave a firm nod to confirm the plan.

Dakota turned her amused features to Barr.

"*But if you don't agree, we'll take you both back to the High Commander, and she will peel your skin off while you're still alive.*" Charlie flashed a toothy smile and taunted, "*I'm sure she'd like a nice Gyr-skin jacket.*" Her right hand crept lower, closer to her belly.

Barr hissed, then yelled, "*You're not in chargggee!*"

"*Actually,*" Charlie argued, "*I still am.*" She snatched the tiny Grasshopper gun from her waistband and pulled the trigger. A loud, strong sound vibration rocked half the room and tossed the kidnappers and the Omega onto their backs. Dakota slammed into the wall behind her and slumped to the floor. Barr also collided with the wall after he dropped his gun midair, but his body protected the Omega from any damage.

Starr hastened across the short distance and collected the Omega into her arms, taking her away from danger. Charlie and Andren checked the unconscious kidnappers' pulses, then removed any weapons. Together, they used Charlie's metal zip ties to bind Barr and Dakota's hands behind their backs. Once done, they went to Starr and knelt in front of the Omega, who still had the bag tied around her neck.

Starr was using a pocketknife to cut the ropes around the Omega's wrists that were behind her back. But when the Omega started fighting her, she had to pull the knife away.

"It's okay. It's okay," Charlie insisted in Kalmarese. "You're safe. We were sent by Kal to free you." She reached for the black bag. "I'm going to get this off your head so you can see us." And be able to take in Andren's familiar Kalmar scent, which would ease the situation further.

Charlie went slow, not wanting to frighten the Omega more. She untied the string under the Omega's chin, then pulled off the bag.

Much of the Omega's dark hair fell around her face until Andren's nimble fingers combed it out of the way. She gulped for air a few times, then gazed up at her saviors. For a moment, she stared at them, but then she turned to Andren. "You're a Kalmar too."

Clearing her throat, Andren worked her jaw a few times, then murmured, "*Ja.*" Her wide-eyed stare mimicked Charlie and Starr's same gawks.

Before them sat the perfect mirror image of the High Commander, but with eyes a shade darker and shorter hair. And in her gaze was fear, confusion, and hints of hope, making them full of life so unlike the High Commander.

Charlie was the first to pull out of her stupor. "My name is Charlie. This is Andren." She then touched Starr's shoulder, which helped break her trance. "And this is Starr. She's going to get those bindings off your wrists."

The Omega gave a faint nod, then leaned forward and allowed Starr to access the bindings. Her entire body shook despite the fact she tried to hold still.

"Can you tell us your name?" Charlie asked.

"Fairlee," the Omega replied. "My name is Fairlee."

Charlie bit her lower lip and was amazed how easy it was for the Omega to reveal her name, as compared to the High Commander. "We're going to get you out of here and back home, Fairlee." She popped up and radioed, "Raakor, we need that ride now."

"On the way. I should be there in a minute."

"Roger that." Charlie watched Starr toss the bindings away, but then she turned to the two kidnappers. "You think they'll fit in the trunk?"

Starr stood up and peered over at the unconscious lumps on the floor. "Probably so." She grinned at Charlie and suggested, "Might have to fold them over a little."

After a shrug, Charlie announced, "We need to go. Can you walk, Fairlee?"

With Andren's help, Fairlee stood and nodded.

Charlie smiled at Fairlee before she peered up at Starr. "Can you handle the kidnappers?"

"*Ja*." Starr first grabbed her weapons, then went over to the kidnappers and tangled her long fingers into the back of their collars, getting a good handle.

"I'll go first, then you two next, and Starr last." Charlie collected her weapons and tossed Andren's dagger and rifle to her. Exiting the holding cell, she scanned for any trouble but found everything quiet, so she followed the same route they'd used to come in, winding through the small base.

Even with the dangerous situation, Charlie's mind kept going over Fairlee's distinct features and what it all meant for Kal and even Kander. From Andren's reaction, it was clear that Andren had no idea that the kidnapped

Omega was related to Kal. On top of it all, Fairlee had been targeted for a reason and held for ransom. However, Charlie doubted Barr, a Gyr, had any clue about Kal's family, much less where to find Fairlee on Kander. Barr had insider information somehow. The sheer idea made Charlie's stomach woozy and her pace increase, needing to return to Kander as fast as possible.

Outside by the landing pad, Raakor was bringing the craft down beside the transporter. Once he shut off the engine, he hopped out and helped Starr with the two unconscious kidnappers.

"I want to get them in the rear locker," Starr said as she and Raakor dragged the kidnappers to the back of the craft.

Turning to Andren and Fairlee, Charlie hooked the back of her neck and mentioned, "We only have four seats in the shuttle. I hope one of you doesn't mind sitting on the other's lap." She assumed they would be most comfortable with each other. Plus Omegas were generally smaller, and Charlie needed to fly the shuttle.

Fairlee nodded and looked at Andren. "We'll be fine."

Upon noticing a soft flush on Andren's cheeks, Charlie decided to walk away and handle prepping the shuttle for everyone. Raakor went to the transporter's open cargo doors and vanished inside.

"What about the heads?" Starr asked when she came alongside Charlie and held an empty bag from the shuttle's locker.

Charlie grumbled and worried about too much weight hurting the vessel's engine during takeoff. However, the broken planet had less gravity pull, and they might be fine.

"Fifteen thousand stills per head, Charlie."

Giving in, Charlie nodded but barked out, "Don't make a mess in the damn locker." She climbed into the shuttle, leaving the door open while she started the engine. She also made sure that oxygen and heat were vented into the locker so the kidnappers survived the flight up to the *Pacifica.*

Poking her head out, Charlie caught Andren and Fairlee's attention. "You both should load up." Once they complied, Charlie spotted Raakor jogging back from the transporter with their empty duffel bag, which prompted her to remove her rifles and stow them.

A few moments later, everyone was loaded into the shuttle's tight confines, and a strange silence filled the cockpit. Charlie focused on lifting off the ground and later ordered her techbit to play easy listening music, hoping to settle everybody's nerves. The flight to the *Pacifica* was short, and everyone disembarked the craft after it docked in the cargo bay.

"Starr, can you and Raakor take care of our two esteemed guests?" Charlie pointed her thumb at the shuttle's rear locker. "Then I'll catch you both in the cockpit."

Starr nodded and met Raakor at the stern of the craft.

"And I'll show you to your quarters," Charlie offered to Andren and Fairlee. She guided them out of the cargo bay and asked, "Do you need any medical attention?"

"I am unharmed," Fairlee assured.

Charlie turned and went down a few corridors, passing the galley and then coming to the row of doors. "This room and this room are open," she said while pointing to them. "Are you hungry or thirsty, Fairlee?"

"I…" Fairlee hesitated but nodded after gathering her strength. "I am many things, but I think I could use a bath after nearly a fortnight."

Charlie softened after she considered everything Fairlee must have gone through since the moment of her kidnapping. "With the solar currents, it'll take about two hours to travel to Kander. You'll have time to shower, eat, and rest."

"I'm sure you are exhausted among other things," Andren added, but even she seemed weary with the dark circles under her eyes.

"There's a shower in your quarters, towels, and a made bed." Charlie pointed over her left shoulder. "And the galley is back that way to your right. Feel free to eat and drink whatever you like." She offered a smile and joked, "Raakor keeps a variety of food."

Fairlee nodded once, then took a breath and mentioned, "I do wish to know more but perhaps later."

"You should rest," Andren insisted.

"I'll return later to check on you both." Charlie stepped between them and started for the cockpit but paused after a step. "Andren, *tah*."

Andren smiled at Charlie and replied, "*Motah*."

Charlie continued on her way and was happy to find Starr and Raakor waiting for her in the cockpit. "Secure the prisoners?" Their miserable lives would fetch them extra stills with the High Commander.

"Chained and locked up," Starr assured.

"How's your flare-up?"

"Nearly gone."

Charlie noticed a difference and smiled at Starr's returned sanity. She took her seat in the captain's chair and went over all the systems. "What's the local time on Kander?" Behind her, she heard Raakor using his techbit.

"Twenty hundred hours," Raakor reported.

"So it's already dark," Charlie whispered while she continued prepping the ship for departure. "We'll probably make it there around twenty-two hundred hours, then it'll take half an hour to get on the ground."

"Radioing ahead is a waste," Starr muttered.

"They'll be waiting for us," Charlie assured. She put the ship into gear after setting the course to Kander. She had to fly the ship past the planet's former rings before they could enter light speed. "You both should get some rest before we get there."

Raakor took the hint and said goodnight to the team. After he left, Starr slid into the copilot's seat and remained too silent.

Once past the rings and gaining distance from the solar system, Charlie switched to Jero and asked, "*Whaaat?*"

"*You know what.*" Starr stretched her long legs under the panel. "*That girl back there is the High Commander's sister.*" She folded her arms and whispered, "*Somebody other than that Gyr set this thing up.*"

"*Probably so,*" Charlie murmured.

"*And it's not our problem, Charlie.*"

Pretending to focus on the flight, Charlie tried working through Starr's opinion. They were mercenaries and not tied to any one planet or society. But like Starr, she had spent many years of her youth on Kander. There were still humans living there that she cared about. After a sigh, she said, "*Maybe I care a little because I did grow up there.*"

"*You survived there like me.*" Starr regarded Charlie, who ignored the stare. "*You know what happens if we get emotionally involved in this kind of shit.*" She tilted her head and argued further, "*The galaxy gods only know how deep and how ugly this could go.*"

Charlie clenched her jaw to hold back from saying whatever came to her mind. She needed to think, and the flight back to Kander had to be enough time for her. Once they were back, she had to make a decision about whether or not to involve herself. The rescue mission was a job that paid well. It wasn't an invite to return to Kander, was it?

Starr shook her head, stood, and started out of the cockpit. Her next words came out firm, grating against Charlie. "*It's only a job.*"

Chapter 9

Raakor took the copilot's seat and said, "*I have the controls. You should take a break.*"

Charlie muffled a yawn, then stood, accepting the offer. She patted his broad shoulder before leaving the cockpit. "*Only forty to fifty more minutes till we're there.*" She decided to check on the two Omegas and knocked on Fairlee's door, but it was Andren who slid it open.

"*Ja?*"

"*Turen,*" Charlie greeted and watched Andren's features soften. She suspected Andren was on guard duty around Fairlee. "I came to check on you both."

Fairlee approached Andren's side. "It's okay," she insisted and squeezed Andren's shoulder. "I'd like to visit with Charlie alone for a while. You should rest, Andren."

Still the soldier, Andren frowned and turned her stoic features to Fairlee.

"Go," Fairlee ordered. "I'll be fine." Her warm smile seemed to disarm Andren.

After a rumbly sigh, Andren nodded and left the room to go to her own quarters.

"Loyal to a fault," Charlie whispered, then entered the room with Fairlee. "Were you able to rest any?" Behind her, the quarters' door resealed itself.

Fairlee took a seat on the foot of the bed. "I laid down after eating but couldn't sleep."

Hearing that Fairlee ate pleased Charlie, and the lack of sleep was expected after the emotional ordeal. Charlie sat in a chair that had been turned away from the table at some point, most likely by Andren. "It'll take some time." The effects from the kidnapping would take noreds, if not longer, for Fairlee to recover from. "Is there anything I can do?"

Fairlee attempted a smile, but her lips trembled. She shook her head. "You have done plenty."

"We'll be at Kander soon." Charlie leaned forward and laced her hands together between her knees. "I will return you to the High Commander as soon as we arrive." She waited to see or hear any scrap of reaction from Fairlee at the mention of Kal. Would Fairlee confirm that Kal was her sister?

"Then you will collect your payment," Fairlee concluded.

"*Ja*, we do have an arrangement." Charlie continued watching every line in Fairlee's soft features, then spotted the bite mark on Fairlee's neck. She was a claimed Omega, who was missed by her Alpha back at home.

"How much am I worth?" Fairlee met Charlie's stare. Like the High Commander, she had similar green eyes, but they were dark and turbulent.

Biting her lip, Charlie weighed both the question's importance as well as the answer's impact on Fairlee. After a deep breath, she replied, "Two hundred thousand stills." She watched the glassiness in Fairlee's eyes become stronger, and guilt chewed away at Charlie's chest. "And a load of darakar," she added. At the mention of the fuel, she thought back to the kidnappers in the field, before Kal sliced them in half. "But she said you were worth more than all the darakar on Kander."

Fairlee shut her eyes, blew out a shaky breath, and trembled for a moment. She raked her fingers through her dark hair and paced her breathing. Kal and she may be identical twins, but they were opposites. Fairlee embodied life and gentleness, while Kal was Kalatas's emotionless puppet. For a moment, Charlie had a glimpse of who Kal might be if she weren't the High Commander.

"You're her twin sister," Charlie whispered after a beat and studied Fairlee's distant features. The desire to comfort Fairlee rooted itself inside Charlie. She grappled with it as much as Fairlee struggled with her own demons.

"Was."

After an audible swallow, Fairlee regarded Charlie again and explained, "My sister left the day Kalatas took control of her." Her declaration lanced through Charlie's thick skin.

Charlie left Kander ages ago, as a kid. To become a mercenary, Charlie learned to not allow herself to get involved with clients. Kal was a client, and Fairlee was cargo and a means to collect Charlie's payment. But Charlie had gone and slept with her client, who fucked Charlie so well. Her night with Kal had been different from Charlie's previous times with other lovers. They had connected on a new deep level. Kal had fucked Charlie as if she had known Charlie and her body for years. Even now, a tingle burned underneath her skin.

Hidden away in this room with Kal's twin, Charlie learned more about the High Commander and how her ascension affected her family. Fairlee seemed to have continued with her life after her sister's departure, but Fairlee was broken by the loss of her sister. Did Kal feel any ounce of love for her sister and family? Or had Kal left her family without remorse to become the High Commander? She and Kal had spoken about Kal's previous life, but Kal's responses had been rote in nature rather than heartfelt.

After a sigh, Charlie argued, "I don't know about that." She moved from the chair and took a seat beside Fairlee. "I spent some time with her. She is Kal but there's still life in her." She watched Fairlee's stricken profile, hoping her words helped somehow. "I think your sister is still in there."

Fairlee covered her mouth and muffled a sob. She dropped her hand to her lap and whimpered before she spoke again. "Sometimes I still feel her, or fragments of her, but then she slips through my fingers." She rubbed her palms together and looked at Charlie. "Do you have a twin?"

"*Joh*. I have no siblings, but I've heard twins have a special connection."

"We always did. Even when she left home, I still knew she was okay," Fairlee explained. "But then it was broken when Kalatas took her."

"But it comes back sometimes?"

Fairlee gave a soft nod.

Charlie toyed with her fingers, trying not to give in to touching Fairlee. She hadn't comforted someone in many years, but Fairlee's pain and love for Kal were palpable. To lose her twin sister, but then feel her again at random, would break anyone. It had to be a constant state of mourning.

After a deep breath, Fairlee spoke again but in a stronger tone. "You care."

"I—" Charlie hesitated from deflecting the truth. She confronted the strange weight inside herself and admitted, "I do care."

Fairlee revealed a slight smile and whispered, "Alphas are completely wrong about Betas."

Charlie bit her lip, remembering how Andren also used the slur name in a pleasant manner as if it were an honor. Omegas seemed to have a different opinion about humans despite the differences between their two races. Dorlon was another Omega, who befriended Charlie during the war. "I've heard humans are now called Betas."

"Earthlings," Fairlee corrected. "Only Earthlings that are on Kander."

There were other humans throughout the galaxy, a few race variants on planets other than Earth. When Charlie's home planet was destroyed, her people traversed the galaxy and settled on two planets, one of which was Kander.

"Other humans do not understand Kalmar," Fairlee said.

After a moment, Charlie shook her head at the notion that Earthlings understood the Kalmar. Perhaps there were more changes on Kander than Charlie knew. There was peace between the Kalmar and the Earthlings, but she doubted there was true acceptance. Yet Fairlee and Andren held no contempt for Charlie or the other Earthlings. "You called me a Beta. How do you know I am one?"

Fairlee tapped her nose once and replied, "I can smell your scent. It's nothing like the humans who held me captive." She grinned when Charlie lifted an eyebrow. "A human from Kander smells different than one not from Kander."

Startled by the information, Charlie combed her hair back and released a heavy breath. "Wow," she muttered. Her scent must carry a marker that indicated her time on Kander. The supposed Beta marker might have helped settle Fairlee's apprehension earlier when they saved her from Barr.

"Why do you care?"

Charlie gave a curious glance and waited for Fairlee to explain herself.

"For Kal," Fairlee added.

"I uh…" Charlie grumbled at her discomfort and weighed the real answer. Why was it so damn easy to talk to Fairlee? "I don't know. I just do." She wiped her damp palms on her worn jeans. "She's different. She's different from any Alpha I've met." In truth, Kal was unique in her own right compared to anyone who Charlie had met over the span of her life. She'd met a variety of people from numerous races in the galaxy.

"She is different from most Alphas," Fairlee agreed.

"She told me she's a Carnec Alpha." Charlie blushed when Fairlee gave her a knowing look, praying that Fairlee had no clue about Charlie's affair with her estranged sister. Hopefully Kal's scent didn't cling to her, or Fairlee would have noticed by now.

"A Carnec Alpha is special and rare," Fairlee said, breaking the tension in Charlie. "A Carnec is only born among identical twins."

Charlie stiffened and tried absorbing the new details. She wasn't aware of Carnec variants among the Alphas and Omegas. Kal had told her the basics, but

Fairlee was offering more information. Had Kal omitted the truth about Carnecs having identical twins so that Charlie wouldn't connect the dots? But how would Charlie not find out the truth after seeing Fairlee for the first time?

"The primary twin is either an Omega or an Alpha while the secondary twin is the Carnec." Fairlee paused when Charlie met her gaze, but she continued explaining the nature behind them. "The secondary twin will be the opposing sign, except they will carry both reproductive organs."

"So," Charlie repeated the explanation, "the secondary twin, which is the Carnec, will be the opposite sign of the primary, have both reproductive organs, but look like the primary twin."

"*Ja*, exactly." Fairlee smiled at Charlie's comprehension. "In my and Kal's case, I was the primary twin, an Omega, so Kal is the Alpha version of me."

"Damn," Charlie muttered. "I never knew this about Alphas and Omegas."

"*Ja*. It is rarely spoken of in Kalmar culture."

"Kal said Carnecs are often killed at birth, especially the Alpha ones."

Fairlee nodded and brushed a loose piece of hair behind her ear. "Thankfully, our parents were proud to sire both an Omega and an Alpha at once."

After a low grunt, Charlie tilted her head and asked, "Do you think Kalatas chose her because she is a Carnec Alpha?" Her conversation with Dorlon had already led her to believe that Kander's god had great plans for Kal.

"Of course." Fairlee lifted her chest and smiled big. "Before becoming Kal, my sister was different from all the other Alphas in the village." She folded her hands in her lap and looked down, as if gazing into the past. "She was both gentle and fierce, like an Omega and an Alpha. Unlike families that had one Omega child and one Alpha child, we were much closer than those siblings, to the point that other pups couldn't understand it."

"They were jealous," Charlie guessed.

"They were scared," Fairlee explained, her smile slipping now. "But my sister held her ground and protected me at every turn."

Charlie imagined a young version of Kal waving a stick around at other kids. She grinned to herself and contained her chuckle. "I guess they were all surprised when she became Kal."

Fairlee laughed, then shrugged and said, "Many don't even know and haven't connected the dots." She sighed and pursed her lips. "She was very young when she left home."

Nibbling on her lip, Charlie weighed her chances to learn Kal's former name, needing the truth to bring her closer to Kal for some reason. Maybe Kal's old name would somehow free one of the many locks that Kalatas had on Kal. Her heartbeat grew stronger, but she gathered herself and asked, "What was Kal's name before she became the High Commander?"

Fairlee lowered her head, as if searching for something or perhaps fighting a demon. Her features twisted in pain, and tears fell down her cheeks.

Unable to withhold herself, Charlie grabbed Fairlee's smaller hand and snaked her arm over shaking shoulders. "Fairlee," she rasped as the pain transferred into her.

Fairlee shook against Charlie and whimpered once, before she confessed, "I don't know her old name." She lifted her grieving features and shook her head over and over. "It was taken from me upon her ascension. It was taken from all of us."

"Oh gods," Charlie whispered and wiped the tears from Fairlee's reddened cheeks. "*Perka gi,*" she apologized.

"I should have written her name down, in the dirt or on a tree, but I didn't know." Fairlee growled and brushed the dampness from her face. "When I know her name again, that's when I'll know. I'll know she's dead."

Charlie swallowed hard against the prickly lump in her throat, keeping her emotions in check. She pulled Fairlee against her and offered all her comfort. For the second time, she cursed Kalatas for taking so much from Kal's family. However, the means justified the ends in the eyes of the god, who needed to rule its people with a clear mind and no personal ties.

"I know she would want you to honor her sacrifice," Charlie whispered and hoped Fairlee would calm down.

"I-I honor it every day." Fairlee trembled against Charlie. "Because, otherwise, I'd mourn the loss of my sister every damn day."

Charlie squeezed Fairlee tighter and bit back on her own pained whimper for Fairlee and for Kal. She gazed up at the metal ceiling and willed herself to wrangle in her emotions. She was being a poor mercenary, but Fairlee's anguish was hard to ignore.

Fairlee pulled away and cleared her throat before saying, "I am proud of her." She attempted to smile while she dried the last of the moisture from her face. "She will be one of the greatest Kals in the planet's history. I know it."

"I think she already is," Charlie declared and mirrored Fairlee's smile. She slid off the bed, then went to the exit and stood near the sealed door. "You should at least lie down for the rest of the trip. We'll be back on Kander soon, and you'll be reunited with your Alpha." When she noticed the relief in Fairlee's eyes, she accepted that the job was about more than stills. Charlie tried keeping her personal emotions at bay, but it was becoming harder, as if Kander's gravity pulled at her soul.

"You should rest as well."

Charlie chuckled, sighed, and allowed her shoulders to droop. "*Ja.* I can feel it." She tapped the button to open the door. "See you soon."

"Charlie?"

Pausing, Charlie peered over her shoulder at Fairlee.

"*Tah.*"

After the thank-you, Charlie shrugged and brushed off the sincerity with a joke. "Just a merc doing her job."

She left without waiting for a reply and went to her own quarters. There was enough time to have a quick nap before she had to return to a tall tower full of damn Alphas, including her favorite one.

* * *

"*You're not going down there alone,*" Starr snarled in Jero and bared her teeth at Charlie.

"*I wasn't asking.*" Charlie kept her back to Starr while she packed a duffel bag for her trip to Tarrak. "*I was telling you.*" She heard Starr's approaching steps and felt the overwhelming presence loom over her.

"*I won't let you go down there alone.*" Starr placed a firm hand on Charlie's shoulder. She was always Charlie's protector, ever since she joined the crew.

Sighing, Charlie turned around and narrowed her eyes. "*We might seem like partners, but we're not.*" The sting in Starr's features filled her with regret, but she held her position. "*This is my ship, and you are part of my crew.*" She leaned in closer and declared, "*You follow my orders or get off my boat.*" Ignoring Starr's hurt, she demanded, "*Are we clear?*"

"*I'm only—*"

"*Are we clear?*" Charlie cut her off.

With nostrils flared, Starr released a huff, yanked her hand free, and replied, "*Yes.*"

Charlie willed Starr to leave her quarters and watched her exit the room. Once alone, she rubbed her brow but continued packing a few items in case she ended up on Kander for a night.

Secretly, she wished to stay in hopes that she and Kal would fuck again. Such thoughts took her back to the drawers that held her clothes and other belongings. In the lower left drawer, she dug through a few pairs of jeans until she located one of the sex toys. Lifting her hand, she hummed at the soft, pliable ring and smirked when her moving thumb triggered it to wake up. The Red Cherry Ring was a toy that Charlie hadn't used yet, unsure when she'd have a partner for it. After a tick, she decided it was worth taking even if the chance of using it was slim.

Once finished in her quarters, Charlie took the overnight bag to one of the shuttles and put it in a back seat, noticing Raakor hunched over the open locker. He shut the lid after loading two kidnappers inside it.

"*Are they sedated?*"

"*Yes, you should be safe,*" Raakor promised. "*The heads are also in there.*" He approached Charlie and asked, "*Are you sure about going by yourself?*"

"*I'll be fine.*" Charlie saw Raakor's easy acceptance, unlike Starr. "*I may return in a few hours or at dawn.*"

Raakor folded his arms, showing off his purple biceps due to his black tank top. "*With a full account of stills.*" He then frowned and muttered, "*I suppose that means a celebration at Lerto?*"

Charlie laughed and patted his shoulder.

"*We will need to fuel up at Lerto,*" Raakor admitted.

"*Actually, the High Commander promised the load of darakar to us after we completed the mission.*" For the first time, Charlie watched Raakor's eyes bulge, and she laughed at him. "*We'll be set for a while.*"

"*Yes,*" Raakor murmured and scratched his chin. His technical mind probably was trying to fathom how long the darakar would last them. The special fuel could burn long and slow in any engine.

"*I need to go.*" Charlie went in search of the two Omegas that were due back on Kander. She found them both in Fairlee's room, so she guided them to the bay where Raakor still waited for them.

"*Tah* for your help," Fairlee offered to Raakor, who bowed his head and gave a slight smile. She then loaded into the shuttle's copilot seat while Andren sat in the back.

"*I have my techbit,*" Charlie told Raakor. She hopped into the pilot's seat and prepared for departure while the doors closed and locked themselves. "This'll be a quick ride down but might be a little bumpy. From the scans, it looks like there's some rain moving in."

"How bumpy?" Andren asked.

"Nothing serious," Charlie lied. She ignored Fairlee's inquisitive glance and waited until Raakor left before opening the bi-door of the bay. Once cleared, she maneuvered the vessel out and into outer space, then flew to Kander, aiming for Tarrak. Once within range, she radioed the planet and grinned when she recognized the voice.

"*Tah*, Blade Perras," Charlie replied over the radio channel and pictured his dumb look. She slowed the craft once they entered the planet's atmosphere. The gradual increase of gravity started to pull the ship downward.

As the shuttle ate away at the marches, they entered a lower layer of the planet's atmosphere that had an ugly, cold storm front moving through it. The fuselage shook from the turbulence, then the shuttle bounced up before it dipped fast. Fairlee latched onto the front dash and missed hitting a few switches. Several more times, the shuttle dropped in altitude before lurching up again from strong wind drafts.

Fairlee yelped each time and clutched her stomach.

"I thought you said it was nothing serious!" Andren growled and slapped her hands against the shuttle's overhead fuselage.

Charlie was concentrating on the flight but remarked, "I've had worse." She checked the navigation screen to ensure she was on target for the same landing spot as last time. "It'll settle down in a tick." Once the craft passed through another layer of the atmosphere, the ride smoothed out and the bumps lessened.

"Tell me it's not much longer," Andren pleaded.

After a laugh, Charlie teased, "I thought you liked being a space merc."

"I prefer being a soldier on Kander."

Charlie grinned, then shook her head. "I was going to offer you a job on my ship." She chuckled when Andren grunted in response. Her attention returned to the flight, and she saw they had three marches left before they were on the ground. She needed a little inspiration for the landing, so she ordered, "Nova, play my Badass Mix list. Start with 'I Want to Come Over.'"

"Playing your Badass Mix list."

Over Melissa Etheridge's singing, Fairlee asked, "Do you always listen to music?"

Charlie flashed a grin, then replied, "Most of the time, but especially when I land a ship." She tapped the touch panel and turned on the landing lights, knowing it would stir up the Kalmar soldiers on the ground who waited for them. Refocusing on the instruments, Charlie sang alongside Melissa Etheridge and put her heart into both the song and the landing.

The craft's nose lifted and slowed the rapid descent to the ground. After it banked to the right, it flew north a ways while it continued closing in on the landing spot. Then Charlie banked the shuttle to the left when they came over the top of the spot. She kept it tilted at a certain degree and spiraled downward to the ground for a minute before she landed the shuttle without a hitch.

There were several pained moans in the cockpit that made Charlie laugh. She turned off the music and announced, "After the engine shuts off, you can get out or fall out if that's easier."

Andren grumbled from the back.

When the automatic doors lifted, Charlie exited, and fine droplets of rain dusted her clothes and face. "Great," she muttered. From both the shuttle and the vehicles' lights, she made out the dark figures circling them.

Andren went around Charlie but paused when Fairlee came to them on one side of the craft. Charlie remained still, quiet, and waited this time for whoever was in charge.

Commander Gaveston emerged in front of them, still as stone-faced as ever. Two soldiers flanked him on either side with their rifles ready. "We will take the Omega from here, and you can return to your ship until Kal contacts you."

Narrowing her eyes, Charlie neared her hand to the gun holster in her jacket. "I don't think so." She shifted in front of Fairlee, blocking Gaveston and the nearing soldiers. "I will take her to Kal myself."

Gaveston bared his teeth and lifted his hand, about to signal the soldiers, but never made the call. His attention had shifted to Andren, who aimed her laser rifle toward him. He recovered from his initial shock and snapped, "Move, Omega."

Andren opened her mouth, but it was cut off by another Omega's voice that came from the darkness.

"Stand down, everyone." Commander Dorlon emerged in the streams of light, appearing calm. "Charlie only wishes to complete her job and personally return the Omega to Kal." She gave Gaveston a dangerous smile and ordered, "We will honor her wishes."

Gaveston lowered his arm, then nodded before he ordered the soldiers to load into the vehicles.

Dorlon remained in charge and escorted Charlie, Andren, and Fairlee to a hover truck, then climbed last into the truck bed. After her signal, they drove through the light rain that added a slight chill to their bones. The view of the Great Tower was a welcomed sight, and the torch-lit walkway guided them into the tower's grand foyer, which was buzzing with activity.

Charlie was on Fairlee's left side while Andren was anchored on the right. Together, they escorted Fairlee through the entrance and found the crowd parting, funneling them to one person in the center of the foyer. The High Commander was in her usual black attire, long coat, and boots. She held her hands in front of herself and raised her chin when Charlie approached her with the kidnapped Omega. All around them, the people whispered among themselves, but Charlie couldn't catch any of it.

After a deep breath, Charlie halted them a few paces in front of Kal and presented Fairlee to her. "As promised."

Kal's attention flickered to Fairlee, then locked on Charlie again. "*Ja*, it is done." She signaled the guards on her left and ordered, "Take the Omega and lock her in a room for the night."

The three guards marched forward but faltered when Charlie blocked their path. They tightened their grips on their spears, ready to use them at any moment.

"Is there a problem?" Kal demanded, her thick voice echoing off the walls.

"Charlie," Fairlee whispered, "it's okay." She touched Charlie's arm and used her pheromones to cool Charlie's rising temper.

Charlie looked sidelong at Fairlee and saw her calm manners. Fairlee was *safe* here, especially in the Great Tower of all places. Next to Fairlee, Andren had a pleading expression that undid the rest of Charlie's protective response. After a swallow, she returned to her original spot and replied, "*Joh*, Kal."

Kal nodded at the guards, who followed their orders. She waited until the guards were gone before she said, "You will be paid in full at first light. Until then, you may stay as a guest or return to your ship."

Biting on the inside of her mouth, Charlie gazed over at the guards who escorted Fairlee up the steps to the elevator. She then turned back toward Kal and mentioned, "I have two kidnappers in my shuttle along with several heads."

"And I will honor our terms," Kal assured.

"I will stay in Tarrak tonight." Charlie noticed how Andren straightened.

"You are dismissed from duty this evening," Kal ordered Andren. "Return to the barracks and rest."

Ever the soldier, Andren bowed her head in submission.

"Commander Dorlon will take you to your shuttle for the kidnappers." Kal signaled Dorlon to come forward. "And we will complete our deal at first light." With her final word, the public meeting came to a sharp end, and everyone spoke at once.

Dorlon darted over to Charlie but looked at Andren and reminded, "You are dismissed."

"*Ja*, Commander." Andren exchanged a glance with Charlie before she vanished among the people.

Charlie tried to grab Kal but was blocked by Dorlon. She glared and said, "I need—"

"Let it go," Dorlon warned. "And don't speak any further here." Similar to Andren, she seemed to be protecting Charlie from making a mistake.

Charlie ground her teeth and struggled with her irritation. How could Kal ignore her twin sister in such a manner? Over Dorlon's shoulder, Kal spoke to Lennox and was facing in Charlie's direction. However, Kal didn't acknowledge Charlie, as if she was unimportant. It'd been only days ago that she and Kal had shared a special night. Charlie believed their night together had at least nudged them past a client and mercenary relationship.

Dorlon snared Charlie's shoulder, pushed, and ordered, "Go." When Charlie shrugged off her grip, her next words held warning in them. "Don't be stupid right now."

Charlie cracked and turned on Dorlon. "That Omega was—"

"Don't." Dorlon held up a finger between them. "Not here. Not now." Fire lit her eyes with wildness. "Go."

Charlie cussed, then stormed off and left the Great Tower. Her deep huffs formed in the cool night air. The rain attempted to wash away the hard lines on her face while she stomped down the walkway to the trucks. Dorlon came to Charlie's side and remained quiet. Once in the truck bed, they stared across at each other in a silent battle of wills. Certain things hadn't changed between them, even though years had gone by.

The ride to the shuttle and back to the city took an hour, but it did nothing to settle Charlie's anger about Kal ignoring her sister. She fumed during the whole ride to Tarrak and felt Dorlon's stare pinned on her. Once back at the Great Tower, Charlie jumped out of the truck with the duffel bag and was escorted up to the floor with guest rooms.

Dorlon remained on Charlie's heels.

After walking around, Charlie deduced which room was hers, since it had an Alpha guard. She saw three guards at another door farther down, and it dampened her mood again.

Dorlon followed Charlie into the room and slammed the door. "What were you thinking, you idiot?"

Charlie tossed the bag onto the bed, then turned her wrath on her old friend. "She didn't even acknowledge it was her sister!"

"Because that Omega isn't her sister anymore!" Dorlon neared Charlie and held her ground. Their arguments during their childhood had been similar, each of them matching the other. "She is simply another citizen of this planet like all the rest of us."

"I don't believe that for a damn tick. She wouldn't have hired me if it wasn't her sister." Charlie threw her hands in the air. "If Fairlee didn't still mean something to her." She rubbed her brow, which started to hurt from her scowl.

Dorlon shook her head and countered, "It didn't matter whether it was her sister or another; she would have done anything to retrieve one of her people." She narrowed her eyes and whispered, "All the time you've spent here, and you've not learned a damn thing about the High Commander."

"You mean that last fucking knothead who nearly wiped my people out?" Charlie fired back.

"Your people?" Dorlon laughed without a hint of humor. She stared with her jaw loose before she spoke in a growly tone. "Since when did you give two fucks about your people?" She snatched the collar of Charlie's jacket and jerked her into her body. "Kal has given away everything, so she could save *your people*." She bent over until their lips were scant inches from each other. "At least give her the respect she deserves." After she shoved away Charlie, she moved to the door but turned around when Charlie spoke.

"*Ja*, she gave away everything and lost what made her a Kalmar." Charlie trembled, but she was unsure if it was from the fight or how close Dorlon had been to her. Had Dorlon been tempted to kiss her? "How is that fair to her, to her sister? Her entire family?"

Dorlon narrowed her eyes and asked, "Why do you even care? You left this planet a long time ago. Nobody is asking you to understand our ways." She faced the door, about to leave.

Charlie struggled with the honesty until she blurted it out. "Because I don't have one." When Dorlon looked at her again, she yelled, "Because I don't have a family, and she threw hers away."

"Don't you think she considered all of that before she looked into the Light?" Dorlon asked and neared Charlie. "It was her choice." Her voice had softened and eased the stiffness in Charlie's shoulders. They were once friends, even family, to each other. She, Dorlon, and Raine had once been inseparable until the war between the Earthlings and Kalmar drove them apart.

"I know. I know that." Charlie patted her pounding heart and blinked away the burn in her eyes. "I didn't have that choice." But then her heart stuttered between beats when Dorlon's face fell.

"*Ja*, you did." Dorlon shook her head and disappointment flashed in her eyes. "You abandoned your family here on Kander, your friends, your people, and me." A hint of disgust lingered in her tone. She huffed and returned to the door, seeming more determined to leave. "You made your choice too, but at least hers was a noble one." Then she was gone, with another boom of the door.

Charlie reversed until the back of her knees hit the bed, then she toppled to the floor and could no longer ignore the tears that had been fighting to escape. She propped up her legs and let the old, ugly emotions drown her until she fell over, exhausted and weak. For once, sleep buffered her from the harsh reality of her choices in life.

* * *

A low vibration started in Charlie's jacket pocket, then an increasing chime forced Charlie to wake up. The room was dark, other than the moonlight streaming through the window. But the annoying noise forced her to sit up. The stiffness in her muscles brought out a groan. She retrieved the techbit and tapped the answer button.

"*Hey, Raakor.*" Charlie had to clear her throat.

"*Hey, boss. Sorry to bother you so late, but a transmission came in.*"

Charlie ran her fingers through her disheveled hair. "*From who?*"

"*From Sallarus,*" Raakor replied. "*He's got a job for us. I told him you'd respond to him soon. He said he'd better hear from you in twelve hours, or he was calling Taj.*"

"*Oh, for fuck sake!*" Charlie rolled her eyes and argued, "*That dickweed couldn't tie his boots, much less do a job right. Did you tell him we're at Kander?*" Without being on the *Pacifica*, she couldn't connect to the Jerothian's communication network that was throughout the galaxy.

"*Yes, I told him we're finishing up a job with the Kalmar. He cooled off then.*"

Charlie smirked. Sallarus would be interested to hear about the job from the Kalmar. She was the first mercenary to receive a job from Kander and its outer-space-hating people. "*I'll be up there tomorrow morning after I get our stills from the High C.*"

"*Understood.*"

After a sigh, Charlie asked, "*How's Starr?*"

"*Licking her wounds but fine otherwise.*"

Charlie hoped Starr was over their argument by the time she returned to the ship. She stood and worked the strain out of her muscles. "*I'll let you know when I'm headed up. But we'll have to come back down with both shuttles for all the darakar.*"

"*Yes, ma'am.*"

Charlie rolled her eyes after Raakor's tease. "*See you in a few.*"

"*Sleep well, boss.*" Raakor ended the transmission first.

Charlie grunted and decided she should at least sleep on the bed rather than the floor. Using the techbit's light, she undressed and wore something lighter for bed. She kept her weapons nearby, but then it occurred to her that they weren't confiscated from her. The Kalmar's lapse in procedures left a bit to be desired. She wondered if it was an oversight or a newfound trust from Kal. Rolling over, Charlie did her best to sleep rather than think anymore about Kal, Dorlon, or the whole damn planet. She would be happy to get off this hellhole again and leave it—for good.

* * *

An hour after dawn, Charlie rose and prepared for the day, which would be rather busy. She had a lot to accomplish before she and her crew could fly away from Kander. The night's rest had improved her overall mood, even if Dorlon's words still stung. Once ready, Charlie shouldered the duffel bag's strap and went to the door, which was being guarded by a soldier on the other side. When she left the room, she noticed that the three guards for Fairlee's room were gone. "What happened to the Omega?" she asked.

The guard adjusted his grip on the spear and replied, "She has been taken."

"To where?" Charlie grumbled when she received no response. She hastened to the elevator and the stupid guard accompanied her. The ride to the ground floor was quiet and a bit awkward, but Charlie toyed with her techbit. Near the building's main entrance, various people chatted, including Fairlee. Charlie bolted down the steps from the elevator lobby and called, "Fairlee."

Turning around, Fairlee smiled. "*Turen*, Charlie." The dark lines under her eyes were gone. At least Fairlee was able to sleep and be ready for her journey home.

"What's going on?"

"I am being escorted back to my village," Fairlee replied.

Charlie bit her lip, then came closer and whispered, "Did you see—"

"*Joh*." Fairlee shook her head. "But it's okay."

Charlie glowered, and a slight burn rose in her cheeks. How could Kal ignore her sister? Last night was an opportunity for the two to reconnect, but Kal let it slip by. Fairlee's delicate touch against Charlie's raised hand cut through her rekindled annoyance. Charlie adjusted her grip on the duffel bag's strap, but it did nothing to break Fairlee's contact.

"Now that I've been returned to my planet, I will be going home soon. Back to my Alpha and my children." Fairlee curled her fingers around Charlie's closed hand and smiled with open sincerity that outweighed Charlie's coming payment. "I am thankful, especially to you."

Charlie looked away and collected herself, trying to steel her emotions. She cleared her throat and nodded at Fairlee, who was supposed to be a payday, nothing else. "I was hired, remember?" Her rebuke did nothing to break Fairlee's smile.

"I am still thankful that you were successful." Fairlee closed the gap between them and offered an open arm. The silent request was there, and Charlie struggled with how to handle the situation.

Charlie dropped her duffel bag to the floor.

Fairlee took her opening and hugged Charlie, who returned it without hesitation. The tenderness and sureness of Fairlee's hold melted Charlie's colder layers. The flicker of affection between them was familiar and welcomed. Charlie had no idea when she last hugged anyone, much less for this long. As Fairlee disentangled, she kissed Charlie's flushed cheek and whispered, "If you do care, give my sister time."

Time to do what?

Before Charlie could voice her question, a raw type of power flooded the area around them. She was familiar with who possessed such energy and turned to see the High Commander approaching them.

Kal had narrowed eyes and stared at Charlie and Fairlee, but then her face returned to its normal impassiveness. Behind her were nine soldiers who stood with straight backs and firm grips on their metal spears.

Charlie folded her arms and waited for whatever Kal wanted from them.

"You will be returned to your village in Kardos," Kal said to Fairlee. Charlie sharpened at the mention of the northern province, but held her tongue rather than interrupt the ruler. "Twelve soldiers will escort you." She signaled for the nine Alphas behind her to join the other three at Fairlee's side. "Safe travels back home."

Fairlee bowed her head and said, "*Tah*, Kal." She glanced at Charlie one last time, appreciation shining in her eyes. Taken from the lobby, she left the Great Tower.

Charlie watched Fairlee and sent silent well wishes for her. For a moment, she had met the High Commander's sister and had a peek at who Kal once was. Turning on her boot heels, she gazed up at Kal, who was staring at her.

"You are late again for our meeting."

"Right," Charlie murmured and struggled to keep her tone even. "Just a slight oversight." Punctuality appeared to be at the top of the High Commander's list. It wouldn't matter once Charlie collected her payment and left Kander.

Kal gave a hum that rumbled low. "We will complete our transaction in my office." She dismissed Charlie's guard, leaving them alone.

Kal's promise sent a shock through Charlie's belly and settled in her gut, making her clit throb. She grumbled at her lack of self-control around Kal. She refocused herself by picking up the overnight bag, then said, "After you." Kal led them to the elevator lobby on the second floor.

Charlie stood next to the High Commander while they waited for the elevator. She vibrated with the urge to bring up Kal's twin sister but contained herself until they were truly alone. Once in the elevator, Charlie toyed with the shoulder strap and worked up the nerve.

Kal stared at the sealed gate of the elevator, calm as ever and as if Charlie wasn't present. Her hands were linked in front of her body in her usual stance.

"Did you even speak to your sister before you sent her away?" Charlie asked. Somehow she kept a stammer out of her voice despite the fact her entire body quaked and tensed. She expected Kal to turn on her, but a weighted silence hung in the elevator.

After a minute, Kal turned her head and stared at Charlie. The blankness of her expression stabbed Charlie, but Kal's robotic response wedged the blade deeper. "A god has no family."

With closed eyes, Charlie measured her breaths and talked herself down, to be logical rather than irrational about the situation. After a deep breath, she opened her eyes and mentioned, "Well, somebody out there got the impression she's your twin sister and had her kidnapped for a reason." She tilted her head and watched Kal. "My guess is that Gyr had no idea you have or had a sister. Somebody told him."

Kal remained silent and returned to staring at the elevator's locked gate.

"Aren't you even the least bit worried that somebody is trying to get at you?"

When the elevator hitched, Kal worked the gate free. "It does not concern you. Your job is complete." She stepped off the lift now that the gate was open, then went to the office.

"In, out," Charlie coached herself and paced her breathing while following Kal. Once in the office, she dropped the bag near the door and waited until Kal closed it. "But it might be my job again if they decide to kidnap somebody who's valuable to you, like Dorlon."

"Then you should be happy to receive another job," Kal concluded. She went behind the desk and collected the folded tablet that had been charging in the sunlight. Her attention was on the tablet, opening it up to its full screen. "Why do you care?"

Looking up to the ceiling, Charlie counted to ten in hopes it would defuse her growing annoyance. She hated being questioned about why she cared about someone or something. Did she have a tattoo across her brow saying she didn't give a shit about anything? She rubbed the spot in case there was one. Her delay in replying seemed to be a prompt for Kal to continue her monologue.

"You left my planet many years ago." Kal tapped on the screen and leaned against the corner of the desk in Charlie's direction. "I called you back here because you are the only mercenary who is familiar with my people." She lowered the tablet to her knee and gazed over at Charlie. "And your job is done, the stills are now in your account, and you may go. I will have the darakar brought to you."

Charlie bobbed her head and looked over to the left, trying to grapple with the tightness in her chest. Their one night together seemed to hold no importance to Kal. After everything, Charlie was defined by her position as a callous merc.

Kal placed the tablet onto the desk and folded her arms. Her gorgeous biceps were on display against the taut jacket. "You hate this planet and my people. Perhaps even your own people."

"I don't hate any of it!" Charlie clenched her teeth and loathed how Kal and Dorlon continued to ram reminders down her throat about how she viewed Kander.

Her eyes glistened with fire, and bitterness crept into her voice. "I hated the war and death."

Kal pushed off from the desk and came to Charlie, studying her with her bright green eyes that bore into her soul. "What is it you truly want if not the stills and darakar?"

"I don't know!" Charlie turned her head away and took a deep breath. She crossed her arms and shifted them a few times. This time, she spoke in a calmer voice. "I don't want anything. I just…" She shook her head and peered up at Kal.

Kal moved into Charlie's space and hooked her chin with a finger, holding their gazes together.

Somehow Charlie was soothed by looking into those godly eyes and being so close to Kal again. The Alpha scent around Kal was earthy and spicy, easing Charlie's defenses. She released a strained breath and backed away from the mental ledge that she'd been walking on for a day.

"You still care after all this time," Kal whispered. "Kander is drawing you back."

Charlie flinched after Kal spoke the truth. She pulled away and backed up a step. "My place is in space," she insisted, hoping to remind herself why she left in the beginning. She needed to have her head examined and realized that Starr was right. This was a job, and getting sucked into anything more was creating a game in her head.

"Perhaps, but Kander will pull you back and maybe sooner than you think."

Charlie huffed before she reached into her pocket and checked her account for the stills. "I do care," she admitted and looked up from the techbit. "I grew up here, and maybe some part of me still sees it as home." She glanced at the deposit in her account and smiled smugly at the number, then reported, "Four hundred and ten thousand stills."

"As agreed," Kal said. "And I will have Dorlon take the darakar to your shuttle."

Charlie locked the techbit and returned it to its home. "I plan to fly up to the ship, then come back with both my shuttles and some muscle." In truth, she wanted to make a transmission to Sallarus before she missed out on another job.

"I will inform Dorlon."

After struggling with herself, Charlie moved closer to the door. "You should watch your back because somebody is targeting you."

Kal neared Charlie again, standing in front of her. "Even if they succeed, my spirit cannot be killed and will move on. They cannot win."

Charlie pursed her lips for a moment, then reached up and pressed her hand against Kal's chest. "But there's still a heart beating under here."

"There are many hearts beating on this planet."

"And every one of them is valuable, including this one," Charlie whispered, hoping that somehow the Alpha behind the god was hearing her. "A true god would understand that."

Kal lowered her head closer, taking deep breaths. A low purr started in her chest and called out to Charlie. She raised her hand and placed it over Charlie's own. "We will meet again," she whispered into Charlie's ear.

Smiling at the promise, Charlie enjoyed their closeness even though their hands were the only contact. Every fiber in her wanted to go to Kal, lean into the skilled hands, and drown in the passion between them. She buried the needs but made the mistake of looking into those greenish-brown eyes. Screwing the damn risk of crossed scents, Charlie rocked up onto her toes and jerked Kal's head down with her free hand.

Kal was stiff when their lips crashed together, but she growled when Charlie nipped against her bottom lip. After running the tip of her tongue across silky skin, Charlie released Kal's swollen lip. She kept a firm hand at the back of Kal's neck and whispered, "That's how humans say goodbye." She swept away from Kal and reached for her bag until she was shoved against the door. Her next breath hitched when her back connected with the hard surface. Already her clitoris throbbed from her lover's rough response.

Kal blocked any escape by placing both hands on the door, on either side of Charlie. Her ragged breaths grazed Charlie's hot cheek. Kal's eyes were blown from rising desire. However, her self-control was strong enough, because she kept their bodies separate so their scents wouldn't mix anymore.

"There is something you must know before you go."

With her hands behind her, Charlie dragged her nails against the door's wood. How she wanted to throw herself into Kal and kiss her again. "What is it?"

"It is something you must take with you into space," Kal insisted.

Leaning in a little, Charlie waited for the special secret and promised, "I will." A storm flickered in Kal's eyes, tempting Charlie to touch her. "What is it?" she urged in a soft voice.

"The morning after we were together was when I remembered, while I stood on the balcony alone." Kal was lighter, as if the god's dark spirit had been peeled away from her very body.

Charlie shook her head and asked, "Remembered what?"

"My old name," Kal whispered, but her voice was hoarse. Her gaze searched Charlie's features with careful and tender assessment, as if Charlie was worth more than the greedy mercenary that she was. Charlie fought to not shake the old name out of Kal, yearning to learn more about the person Kal once was. A brief smile ghosted across Kal's lips, and Charlie thought she imagined it. "My name was Sumner."

Charlie felt her jaw loosen. She fisted her hands and resisted the frenzied urge to kiss Kal. Her heart was thundering in her ears, and a sharpness formed at the back of her throat. She blinked against the growing burn in her eyes. Kal trusted Charlie with her old name.

How can she trust someone like me?

"They say if something goes to space, to the stars, then it will last forever." Kal's ruler mask had faded and someone else was regarding Charlie. There was an Alpha, an emotional being, shackled inside the High Commander. Charlie had sensed it before, but she saw proof today. If she could reach through the thick layers, she might touch Sumner. Kal's rumbly voice recalled Charlie from her thoughts. "*Krafka*, Charlie. Take it with you because I will lose it again."

"I will." Charlie flexed her jaw and willed herself to not shed a tear. She might care to a degree, but she refused to let herself become entangled with anyone again. People die, and death has a price.

Kal bowed her head until their foreheads met in a tender moment. "*Tah*, Charlie," she murmured, and relief was evident in the slump of her shoulders. The tense air fizzled out and left a serene connection between them.

Charlie shut her eyes and absorbed their closeness. She breathed in Kal's heady scent and realized she would miss the comfort of it. Somehow a whimpered escaped her, but she covered it up by swearing, "I promise you, Sumner."

Epilogue

The shuttle drifted into the *Pacifica*'s bay and hovered over its usual docking location next to the second craft. Charlie switched on the magnetic anchoring system that drew the vessel down to the bay's hull. While she shut down the shuttle's systems, the bay pressurized and filled with oxygen, and a rush of hot air warmed the room.

Charlie stepped out but left the pilot's door open since she, Starr, and Raakor would return to Kander for the darakar. Hopefully all the crates would fit in both shuttles; otherwise, a second trip would be necessary. For the rare fuel, it was worth any number of trips and would save Charlie thousands of stills over time.

But first, Charlie needed to call Sallarus and find out what job he had for them. If Lady Luck was with them, then it would be a quick, easy job. Grinning to herself, she became excited to start another adventure soon rather than surviving on empty. As she passed the galley's open door, she noticed a metal mug and plate with half-eaten food sitting on the counter. She hummed low and ducked into the galley, finding nobody around but knowing it was Starr's usual breakfast but half gone. Touching the mug, Charlie frowned at the coolness of the tea and found it rather strange. Starr was neat and tidy in the galley and never left out dishes or food.

Charlie left the galley and approached the cabins, noticing the serenity of it all. She tapped on Starr's quarters first and called in Jero, "*Starr, I'm back!*" After no answer, she picked up the pace and beelined to the cockpit. "*Raakor?*" she yelled while walking the short bridge to the cockpit.

An odd electrical pop forced her to sprint the rest of the way until she nearly collided with a swinging head that was tied to the top of the fuselage. Charlie ducked but slipped on something wet and toppled to the floor. She slid farther until a slumped body stopped her from hitting one of the cockpit seats. In front of Charlie was the decapitated body of Raakor.

"*By all the gods of the universe,*" Charlie murmured, and alarms rang in her head. She reached for her handgun, then jumped to her feet, close to falling from all the blood smeared across the metal floor. Looking over her shoulder, she confirmed it was Raakor's head swinging back and forth, red droplets falling from it. "*No. No. No!*

No! N-n-no!" Her heart fell into her gut before it started pounding.

"*Starr!*" Charlie took a cautious step toward the bridge until a sharp beep from the cockpit caught her attention. She peered over the pilot's chair and grew wide-eyed when a single word popped up on the panel. It simply read "RUN" in bright red letters, then it vanished after a minute and was replaced by a smaller "RUN" in the upper left corner of the panel, followed by a second one, then a third, and one after another until the panel was filled with the word. Like a virus, it spread to the copilot's panel.

"*What the fuck is going on?*" Charlie growled and moved between the chairs, but she paused when the screens went black again. Another loud beep echoed in the cockpit, and then the time 1:53 filled both the pilot and copilot's screen. After a moment, it started counting down at one Earth second, closing in on zero. At 1:45, the *Pacifica*'s internal alarms sounded throughout every deck, and the soft lights turned bright red.

"*Self-destruct sequence has been initiated. Time until self-destruct is one minute and forty seconds,*" the *Pacifica*'s computer announced over the audio system.

"*What?!*" Charlie jumped into the pilot's seat and tapped the touch panel, but it continued counting down. "*Fuck, no!*" She made a few other attempts as the seconds continued winding down closer to self-destruction.

"*Sixty seconds until self-destruct.*"

"*Fuck!*" Charlie screamed and jumped out of the seat, rushing from the cockpit. "*Nova, connect to the* Pacifica*'s system.*" She took a step onto the bridge, sliding on the blood but catching herself with her hands against the ship's fuselage for balance.

"*Connected,*" the techbit reported from the leather jacket's pocket.

"*Begin procedures to start Shuttle One. Download all ship logs and surveillance from the last thirty hours,*" Charlie snapped while her legs danced across the wet floor.

"*Proceeding to start Shuttle One.*"

Sliding past the blood, Charlie ran at top speed yet faltered by the living quarters. Her frantic mind tried deciding whether to duck into her room. She slapped the reader that unlocked the door and drew it open. Rushing inside and heaving for air, Charlie scanned the quarters until she spotted the one item that meant more than the ship itself.

"*Forty seconds until self-destruct,*" the *Pacifica* announced.

Cursing, Charlie took two wide steps, jumped onto the made bed, hopped off, and landed in front of the built-in drawers. Jerking open the top drawer, she tossed clothing items, ignoring the *Pacifica*'s next self-destruct callout. She snatched the precious item that always remained so buried among her belongings and her past. After pocketing it, she bolted through the room and down the halls, adrenaline making her launch across the bay.

The craft hummed with life and hovered above the metal floor with its pilot door still open. Charlie scrambled inside, flicked the switches, and signaled the bi-door to open to outer space. Her seat restraint was forgotten.

"*Logs and surveillance downloaded,*" the techbit stated.

"*How much time until self-destruct?*" Charlie barked and shifted the engine into reverse even though the bay doors were half open.

"*Twenty-three seconds until self-destruct.*"

Charlie jammed the throttle in and forced the shuttle out of the bay, striking the top of the airframe against the upper door. "*Come on!*" Rotating the craft, she skimmed past the *Pacifica*'s hull side and slammed the throttle in again. "*How much time?*" she demanded from the techbit.

"*Eighteen seconds until self-destruct.*"

At full throttle, the shuttle moved as fast as old planes in Earth's atmosphere, but it wasn't fast enough in Charlie's mind. Making it out of the *Pacifica* was no guarantee she was safe once the explosion rippled through space. Regardless of the distance in the next eighteen seconds, the shock wave would hit her, but Charlie knew she had a chance if she aimed for Kander rather than deep space.

"*Time?*" Charlie demanded as she watched Kander grow larger, about to swallow her. The planet's atmosphere had yet to take hold. Sweat beaded across Charlie's brow, then her palms grew slippery against the control stick.

"*Four seconds until self-destruct.*"

"*Fuck!*" Charlie started to pant and wiped her face, breathing harder as the seconds counted down. "*Please. Fates, please.*" She might have a heart attack before the explosion killed her. Desperate for a distraction from her pending fate, she yelled, "*Nova, play Oldies list and start with 'Holding Out for a Hero.'*" Grabbing the seat harness, she hastened to buckle herself in before it was too late.

"*Playing Oldies list.*"

Then, a bright light flickered in the rear camera and blossomed outward until it filled the screen on the dash. The flames plumed and signaled the start of the explosive shock wave that surged and billowed out into space.

Charlie wrapped both damp hands around the controls and clenched her teeth, knees bracing against the consoles around her. "*Please, please, please,*" she chanted.

The silent, unseen tidal wave latched onto the shuttle and launched it forward into Kander's atmosphere, sending everything into pure chaos. For a brief instant, the shuttle surfed the wave until it crashed over the tiny metal cocoon and sent it tumbling into the atmosphere. Gravity gnawed at the hull sides, pulling and clawing at it, then forcing even more speed.

Charlie's scream overpowered Bonnie Tyler's voice, and she attempted to fly the craft as it flipped end over end. The contents of her stomach pitched up, but she held it together. The massive energy wave blew past her into the deeper parts of the atmosphere. For one moment, it seemed safe, until everything was too quiet. There wasn't even the slightest hum from the engine, and again Charlie's heart dropped into her stomach.

"*Shit!*" Using the touch panel, Charlie attempted the reboot signal for the engine, but it wouldn't respond. "*Come on! Restart!*" Without it, the shuttle would be left to freefall to the planet, and with very little control. There was a slim chance she could land it without the engine.

Cussing, Charlie slapped the dash a few times until her anger was extinguished from her veins. After two deep breaths, she started coaching herself, "*You can do emergency landings.*" First, she used the stick to lift the shuttle's nose and slowed the climbing airspeed before the airframe started melting away. Gravity was growing stronger, and it dragged the ship downward faster. From the navigation side of the panel, there were about ten marches to go before she made it to the ground. With a deep breath, she paced herself on the flight down to Kander.

Everything was smooth until an unexpected secondary energy surge lunged at the gliding vessel, grabbing it and hurling it toward the planet's surface. With the nose pointed toward the ground, the shuttle screamed through the atmosphere, then began spiraling out of control. In a corkscrew pattern, the craft dove to Kander with no regret and no control.

Pure fear coursed through Charlie's blood and tried to seize her heart as the green landscape above her head spun closer to her. Her cry filled the cockpit while she fought against the uncontrolled spiraling dive to death. With all her strength, she wrenched on the stick and tried forcing the shuttle's nose to the horizon. Every single G-force battled her and ate away at her consciousness and muscle strength.

The touch panel reported that two marches were left before the shuttle hit the ground. Inch by inch, the horizon started to rise and crept closer to the shuttle's nose. Hope sparked in Charlie's chest and she prayed, "*Please!*" She switched to Kalmarese and pleaded, "*Krafka*, Kalatas!" He was the only god who could spare her. Screaming for life, she used all her power to pull on the stick, and the back pressure grew weaker.

When the craft reached half a march from the forested terrain, the nose kissed the horizon, and the airspeed bled off but not enough before it skimmed the trees. With tears on her cheeks, Charlie growled and gritted her teeth, ready for one ugly landing. Once the shuttle's belly brushed the first leaves, she screamed and raged for all that had happened to her in the past thirty-two Earth years. If this was her end, she looked forward to seeing her family again.

The trees' first branches smacked the shuttle's nose and smashed into the front window. Metal and wood fought while gravity jerked the crashing vessel into the cold, wet ground. One last thick tree branch pierced through the cracked window and entered the cockpit before the spacecraft plowed into the dirt and grass.

The final slam into a large tree slapped Charlie's head back into the headrest, knocking her out for a moment. Soft water droplets patted her cheeks and stirred her awake again, her vision swimming for several minutes. Everything around her was green and brown, including the thick branch inside the cockpit that had shattered the front window.

Charlie coughed a few times, and pain lanced up from her stomach. She noticed the touch panel was damaged, so she was forced to push the door open herself. When it was halfway up, she tumbled out and crawled through the mud and grass to a nearby tree. After rolling onto her back, she gasped from the hot, white, searing pain flaring through her body.

Using the tree for support, Charlie sat up a little, then peered down at what she knew was in her gut. She laughed at the branch that had pierced her lower left stomach. Blood oozed out and soaked around her shirt.

Charlie laughed with pure bitterness, ignoring the pain it caused her. The irony of her death was too perfect. Of all the ways she envisioned her death, it was never on the planet she'd grown up on and by a damn tree branch in her belly. If nothing else, she was happy to die on such a beautiful planet, rather than in the blackness of space. Gazing up, she smiled at the soft harmony of brown, yellow, and red leaves now that autumn was here.

Yet, tears started spilling and mixing in with the soft rain. She dropped her head against the trunk and sent silent apologies to Raakor and Starr for their brutal deaths. She and her crew were supposed to fly off into space with their stills, not die alone. When the heaviness crept into her bones, she shut her eyes and accepted what the Celestial Fates had in store for her. A welcomed and warm darkness crawled through her head, then seemed to spread through her body. Her last thought was about the only person who had awoken her heart.

And she called, "Sumner."

The End

Titles available in *The Alpha God* Series:

Dancing in the Darkness, Book 1
Come to My Door, Book 2
I, Alpha, Book 2.5
Born to Be Mine, Book 3
I, Finna, Book 3.5
Collecting Stars, Book 4
I, True Mate, Book 4.5
Like a Calling, Book 5
I, High Commander, Book 5.5
My Everything, Book 6
I, Sumner, Book 6.5
An Army of One, Book 7
I, Kalatas, Book 7.25
I, Family, Book 7.75
Running Up That Mountain, Part 1, Book 8

Titles available in *The Kingdoms Of Gyldren* Series:

Of Iron and Gold, Prequel
Of Wulf and Wynd, Part 1, Book 1.1
Of Wulf and Wynd, Part 2, Book 1.2
Of Wulf and Wynd, Part 3, Book 1.3

About the Author

Lexa Luthor is an avid writer and reader of the Omegaverse trope especially F/F pairings. In her books, each main character(s) is a strong-willed female, who navigates difficult situations but always ends up finding love with their mate. Every tale has a twist and is gripping, sexy, and even a bit adventurous.

When not writing, Lexa enjoys binge watching television shows like Game of Thrones, Gentleman Jack, or The L Word. Her other favorite hobbies are playing cornhole, rooting for the Kansas City Chiefs, and laying around the pool in the summer. At times, Lexa finds time to read romances (both dark and fluffy) and great sci-fi books but nothing else can beat a steamy, downright erotic F/F romance with biting, knotting, and slightly possessive love.

Visit her website at LexaLuthor.com for more information and be sure to sign up for her newsletter for the latest release information, bonus material, and freebies.